PUPPET
ON A STRING

ALAN W. STAVES

authorHOUSE®

AuthorHouse™ UK
1663 Liberty Drive
Bloomington, IN 47403 USA
www.authorhouse.co.uk
Phone: UK TFN: 0800 0148641 (Toll Free inside the UK)
        UK Local: (02) 0369 56322 (+44 20 3695 6322 from outside the UK)

Published by AuthorHouse 10/22/2021

ISBN: 978-1-6655-9433-2 (sc)
ISBN: 978-1-6655-9434-9 (hc)
ISBN: 978-1-6655-9432-5 (e)

Print information available on the last page.

CONTENTS

CHAPTER 1

AN ORDINARY MAN

His alarm rang with a shrill chirping sound to signal the start of another new day. Gary Taylor stretched out his right arm and slapped his hand down hard on his alarm clock; the ringing stopped.

Gary opened a bleary eye. His clock read 06:55—time to get up. Gary wanted another half an hour in bed but knew it was time to rise. As he opened his eyes, he noticed a small beam of sunlight streaming through a gap in his curtains. It was like a search light, or more likely, the light of a theatre, lighting a small spot on the stage for the ballerina to perform.

With one eye open and the other closed, he followed the beam of light from the window down on to the stage, but instead of a Ballerina all he found was a discarded sock lying on the floor where it had been left the night before.

Gary Taylor got out of bed. He was nothing special. He was an ordinary man of average height, not exactly slim but not fat either—he had not weighed himself for years. He had short-cropped light-brown hair that was growing grey around the edges.

There was nothing unusual about Gary Taylor apart from the fact that he had an irrational fear of clowns. This has a proper name; it is called coulrophobia. If you talk to Gary it is not clowns that he is afraid of—he has never been scared of clowns—it is magicians that he has the irrational fear of. When he was about seven years old, his mother had a party for him, and they had a magician doing magic tricks. The magician called out Gary to help him; all the other children laughed and clapped at the tricks. Gary thought the other children were laughing at him. He was embarrassed and felt humiliated. He thought that the children were laughing at him because he couldn't work out what the magician was doing. From that day forward he had hated magicians, but his mother had told everyone that his fear was of clowns. So, he has never been to a circus, but Gary has no problems with clowns.

Gary had once been in a long-term relationship, for almost eleven years, with a girl called Vivianne La' Court; but she had got bored of him and his dull life and walked out on him. She just packed her bags and left without saying a word. They had been to university together, and Vivianne had been bowled over by Gary's charm. Vivianne had been studying politics and Gary was doing mathematics. They had been introduced by Gary's flatmate Craig Marksbrow. Vivianne had been a political activist and had been on many demonstrations and would take Gary along with her, but it was not really his scene.

After University, Gary bought a house. It was a small two-bedroom house with a garden at the front and back. It had a driveway with block paving stones that could hold up to two cars, even although he couldn't drive.

Vivianne moved in with him, but it was not what she expected. Gary went to work to pay the bills to run the house; Vivianne wanted to go out every night. Once the bills were paid, if there was anything left, then they could go out. Gary was practical and ran an orderly ship. He had a routine and kept to it; but Vivianne couldn't keep to it, and one day she had enough and just left.

Gary carried on with his life as if nothing had happened, but he missed her and had never found anyone else.

Both of Gary's parents had died. His father was fifty-two and his mother was fifty-four. They had been killed in a motor-vehicle accident around about the time that Vivianne had left him. He had no siblings.

He had just turned thirty-six and was an accountant for the engineering firm Melo Phillips. He had been working for them since he was twenty-one. His records showed that they were in financial trouble. The firm had made an annual loss every year since Nathaniel Watson had left—he had taken several of their staff with him to set up a new company called the Corporation which was on Wellington Street.

Sometimes Gary wished he had gone with them. He had alerted his bosses many times that they were incurring losses that were not sustainable, but they carried on as if nothing was happening, just like Gary had done when Vivianne left him. Now they were almost at crisis point, and he dreaded going in to work in the mornings.

He expected that any day he could walk into work and they would say, "That's it, we're done for," and close the doors for the last time.

Gary got up and got washed and dressed. He popped two slices of bread into the toaster—ritual that he had performed many times before.

Gary lightly buttered his toast and poured himself a cup of tea; another day was about to begin.

Gary walked to work with a long purposeful stride. He called in at the newsagents as he did every day and bought the morning paper. He exchanged pleasant remarks about the weather with the newsagent and left just as he had done for the last fifteen years. Nothing ever changed; life just went on as it always did.

On his way out, Gary glanced at the headline on the paper. It was all about Prime Minister Matthew Fenton being the most unpopular prime minister that the country had ever had. In the popularity stakes, he rated below Margaret Thatcher, Gordon Brown, and Theresa May.

Fenton had brought in Universal Basic Income (UBI) as part of his Citizens Charter. Fenton scrapped all benefits and the state pension and replaced it with a single payment of £200 that everyone over the age of twenty one would receive whether they were working or not, the money from the old benefits schemes would pay for this and to prop it up so that they could fully finance it, The utilities companies for gas, electric, and water were told by the government that they were not allowed to make a profit. Any profit that they made would be used to finance this scheme, together with the money that had been used to finance the old benefits systems. This should then also stop the companies hiking their prices every year.

Critics said that this just made the rich richer and the poor poorer, but Fenton had argued that this stopped people abusing the benefit system, as now everyone got the same amount no matter what their circumstances were. His government had voted it through, but the move had made him unpopular, and he had received many death threats.

Gary read the story as he walked into work. He looked at the photo of Fenton and thought that he saw Vivianne in the background. He had not seen or heard from her since the day she had left him; now she was in this photo. When he took a closer look, he could not be sure if it was her or not, but on first glance, he was convinced it was her. The story now said that Fenton's own party had turned against him, but he refused to go and said that he would sort out the country's woes. There was a short note at the end of the article that said Fenton would be touring the country to drum up support, and it listed that he would be in town in four weeks' time.

Gary Taylor had been at work for about an hour when he was called into his boss's office. Gary knocked on the door.

"Enter," came the call from within.

Gary entered the office. It was not an ornate office, rather smart and functional. His boss, Chris Rothberry, sat behind a large desk. He was not a big man; he was getting on a bit in years and was looking rather weather beaten. His hair was grey and looked like it could do with a good combing. He looked tired and unwell. He motioned for Gary to sit down,

Gary sat in a chair in front of the desk. Chris Rothberry spoke in a croaky voice that at times sounded like he was choking back tears. "It doesn't look good, Gary."

"I've been telling you that for weeks—months even."

"We may have come to the end of the road."

Gary had been telling them, from the figures that he had, that the losses were unsustainable and that they would need to make cutbacks, but hearing the words come from Chris was a hammer blow. It hit him like a bolt from the blue. He realised that Chris was telling him that he was letting him go.

"How long do we have left?"

"The bank has frozen our assets. Today is our last day. You will be paid up until the end of the month."

This was not something he wanted to hear, but he had seen this coming and had even warned them that this would happen. They had ignored the warnings; now it was all over. His bosses had been blind to it just like he had been with Vivianne. The warning signs had been there, and like his bosses, he had chosen to ignore them until it was too late.

Gary went back to his desk and started to clear his things away. He wondered what he would do now. He had been with the firm for fifteen years; he knew nothing else.

As he cleared his desk, he sat for a moment and thought about all the people he had worked with. He tried to work out where it had all gone wrong and if there was anything that he could have done to prevent this happening, but there was nothing he could think of.

He had seen it coming, should he have left earlier rather than wait for the inevitable. It was too late now—the damage was done.

Gary went home. He threw his box of belongings into a corner, sat on the sofa, looked out of the window, and decided that he would go out for a drink. Gary was not a big drinker, but this had been a bad day, and so a drink was called for.

Gary went to the Red Lion. This was an old-fashioned public house that, at best, could be called rustic. It was badly in need of refurbishment. It was the nearest pub to where Gary lived, but even so, it was still quite a walk. Gary would often take a shortcut on the old towpath by the canal. It could quite easily be called his local, but he was not a regular.

When he walked in, he wondered why he was there at all. Inside there were only five people in addition to the barman: a local known as Tinky Twinkletoes, three old men that sat in one corner, and a tall blonde woman, who sat in the other corner. The old men were talking in hushed whispers, huddled around a small table. The blonde woman was reading a paper, taking no notice of the others.

Gary ordered a drink and sat with Tinky Twinkletoes. Tinky wore a sparkling-blue jacket and matching trousers with a white fluffy shirt. He enjoyed telling people that he used to be in the ballet in London. Gary had known Tinky for many years but did not know his real name. To Gary, he had always been Tinky Twinkletoes.

"I used to be in the ballet you know."

"Yes, I know.

"Ricardo Futurist was the best ballet dancer we ever had. He said I was too masculine to be a dancer; my lines didn't flow when I danced. Can you imagine that? Me, too masculine to be a dancer?"

"No, that is hard to imagine."

Gary then mentioned Matthew Fenton coming to town, and Tinky seemed to change totally.

"A horrible man Fenton. Do you know what I would do to him?"

"No, tell me—what would you do to him?"

"I would put a gun to his head and blow his brains out."

Gary was shocked by Tinky's sudden outburst of hatred for Matthew Fenton. They sat and talked awhile about politics. When last orders were called, Gary made his excuses and got up to leave. As he reached the door, he looked back into the room. Tinky held an imaginary gun to his head and pretended to blow his brains out. Gary smiled and went home.

Gary took a slow walk home. He walked by the river and along the canal. He walked down the dimly lit old towpath and let the night air clear his head. He slept soundly that night.

CHAPTER 2

THE INVITE

His alarm rang with a shrill chirping sound to signal the start of another new day. Gary Taylor stretched out his right arm and slapped his hand down hard on his alarm clock; the ringing stopped.

Gary opened a bleary eye. His clock read 06:55—time to get up. Gary wanted another half an hour in bed, then realised that he was now out of work and didn't have to get up. He rolled over and went back to sleep. Gary was woken by the sound of knocking on his front door He looked at his clock—it was now after eight. The knocking continued. He went to the door; the postman stood there.

"I have a letter for you; it needs signing for."

Gary signed for the letter. He went into the kitchen, threw the letter on to the table, and put bread into the toaster and water into the kettle. He then sat at the table with his head in his hands, wondering what he should do now, as he no longer had a job to go to.

Gary ate his breakfast and walked down to the newsagent and bought the daily paper.

"You're late today, Mr Taylor."

"Yes, I know."

"Won't your boss be unhappy?"

"No, he fired me yesterday."

"I'm sorry to hear that."

"Me too."

Gary took the paper and went home. He threw the paper on to the table and put the kettle on again. When he returned to the table, he noticed a picture of Tinky Twinkletoes on the front page.

The headline read "Local man attacked last night. Police are appealing for witnesses."

Gary went on to read the paper. The article said that Tinky had been attacked last night, and it was believed to be a politically motivated attack. It stated former ballet dancer Adam Hamilton, better known as Tinky Twinkletoes, was a political activist and was very vocal on his dislike for the Prime Minister Matthew Fenton. He could have been attacked for his outspoken views. They were appealing for witnesses to contact the police.

Gary sat for a long while thinking about last night. Then he decided to go to the police station.

He approached the front desk and spoke to the duty sergeant. "I would like to speak to someone about the attack on Tinky Twinkletoes, please."

"Hold there a minute."

The Sergeant spoke into a phone. Two minutes later, Inspector Leanne Best came through. "I hear you have some information about Adam Hamilton."

"Who?"

"A local man known as Tinky Twinkletoes."

Gary was shocked. He had known Tinky for a long time, but he had never known his real name. Even though he had read it in the paper, he couldn't imagine him as anything other than Tinky Twinkletoes—the name suited him. Inspector Best led him to a small interview room.

WPC Holly Meadows came into the room to take notes. Holly was twenty-four and had been on the force since she left school. She started as a cadet, then had been at the Met for three years before joining Alexander Timpson's new security task force team. Holly Meadows had wanted to be a Ballerina as a child. She was always active, a good dancer, and very sporty. She liked to solve puzzles. She had never thought of joining the police. It was her careers adviser that saw the potential in her—with the puzzle solving—and had recommended that she try out for the police. She joined the police academy as a cadet. On graduating, she spent several years at the Met and made a good impression. When Timpson was setting up his team, her boss recommended her to Timpson. She joined his team on the same day as her colleague Daniel Hobson.

Inspector Best introduced herself and WPC Meadows to Taylor before asking him to sit at the desk.

"Take a seat." Gary sat down. "What do you know about the attack on Adam Hamilton?"

"I know nothing about the attack."

"Then what are you doing here?"

"I was out with Tinky—"

"Adam," Inspector Best corrected.

"I was out with Adam, Tinky, whatever you want to call him, I was out with him last night."

"Till about what time?"

"I went home about eleven-ish."

"Can you be more precise?"

"It was eleven."

"How can you be sure? It was about eleven before, now you are saying it was exactly eleven."

"They call last orders at eleven, and I left when they called last orders."

"Do you have any witnesses?"

"There were a few people in the pub and the barman, but I don't really know any of them, only Tinky."

"What did you talk about?"

"His favourite subject, himself."

"And yet you didn't know his real name."

Gary shook his head almost embarrassed. He had known Tinky a long time but he had always been Tinky Twinkletoes. It had never occurred to him to ask what his real name was.

Inspector Best leaned forward. "Did you see the attack on Mr Hamilton?"

"No, he was fine when I left."

"Did you talk about anything else?"

"Not that I remember."

Inspector Best stood up. "Thank you for coming," she said. "At least we can now narrow down the time of the attack."

"Is that it?"

"Yes, that's it for now. We will call you if we need anything else."

Gary got up and left the room.

Inspector Best went into the next room where Chief Inspector Alexander Timpson was studying a picture board. At the top there was a picture of Tinky Twinkletoes. It listed him as the victim and listed his name as Adam Hamilton. Below him there were pictures of five possible suspects. The fourth one along was Gary Taylor. Below him it said "motive unknown". A blue line linked him to possible suspect number three, Vivianne La' Court. Below her it said "motive political activist; may not have acted alone." In brackets it said "not seen in public for some time."

Inspector Best looked at the wall board. Then chief inspector Timpson spoke. "It's strange that he never mentioned the threat to kill Fenton."

Inspector Best looked at the possible suspects. "Maybe he is hiding something."

"Or protecting someone."

Gary Taylor left the police station. It was a sunny day, and a group of children were playing on the steps. They were singing a song about marching up a hill, and they were pretending to march up the steps; then they marched down again. Gary did his best to ignore them, just in case they wanted money from him.

When he got home, Gary noticed the letter that he had signed for that morning still lay unopened on the table.

Gary Taylor sat at his table staring at the letter. His dad had always told him that any letter you have to sign for will always contain bad news. He twizzled the letter through his fingers, undecided if he should open it or not. The letter was stamped locally. He put the letter back on the table.

Gary made a cup of tea and sat back at the table looking at the letter. He had no idea who it had come from. Eventually his curiosity got the better of him, and he picked up the envelope.

Gary tore the flap open. He tingled with trepidation and anticipation, then he pulled out the letter from inside. It was folded in two. He opened up the letter; in the top right-hand corner there was a stamp indicating that the letter had been sent to him from the Corporation. The address was on Washington Road, which was a little cul-de-sac at the end of Wellington Street. He read the letter slowly. It stated that the Corporation was holding a recruitment drive, and he was invited to come along next Wednesday. The letter was signed by Domenic Clarkson, head of recruitment.

Domenic had worked with Gary at Melo Phillips and had left with Nathaniel Watson.

"Head of recruitment," Gary mused. "Domenic has done well for himself."

Gary had only been out of work for one day, and already he had been to the police station giving a witness statement and had been offered a new job. He wondered if life was like this every day if you were not working.

Thanks to Fenton and his Citizens Charter, Gary was well off and didn't need to rush straight back into another job.

Gary read the letter again. There was no job specification and no mention of a salary.

He wondered what the job would be. He thought that since the invite had come from Domenic, then surely, he remembered him from Melo Phillips, and the job had to be something that Domenic knew this was something that he knew how to do. He read the letter again and noticed there was no contact number on the letter. It looked like, if you were interested, you just had to turn up on the day. Gary thought about it for a moment, then put the letter on the mantle behind the clock—out of sight but just enough showing to remind him that it was there.

Gary went into the kitchen, put the kettle on, and stared out of the window. Then he remembered Tinky saying that he would shoot Fenton. He wondered if the police knew about the threat and if that was what they had wanted him to talk about. Now he was in a quandary and wondered if he should go back to the police station. Should he tell them about the threat that Tinky had made or would this now get him into more trouble?

He paced up and down the room and glanced out of the window. He saw the children marching past his window. Gary Taylor tossed a coin—heads I go back to the police station, tails I stay quiet. The coin came down as heads.

"Best of three," he said to himself and tossed the coin again.

CHAPTER 3

SUSPICIOUS MINDS

Chief Inspector Alexander Timpson carried an air of authority. He was a tall man at six foot four inches; he was forty-six years old. He had joined the police straight from university at the age of twenty-one. He had quickly risen through the ranks to chief inspector, he now ran a special unit on counter terrorism and home security.

His current mission was to make sure that Prime Minister Fenton's tour went ahead with no hitches, but intelligence reports suggested that this was not going to be an easy task. Already, there were a couple of movements out there that wanted to remove Fenton, by fair means or fowl.

Chief Inspector Timpson had a secret dossier that contained leads on key members of groups that were opposed to Fenton. These came from intelligence reports gathered by his predecessor, Cameron David. Alexander Timpson studied the reports. He wondered where Gary Taylor fitted in: true, he had links to all the other suspects, and Taylor had never shown any radical tendencies, but then, he had never been unemployed before. Who knew what may turn a man.

He watched out of the window as Gary Taylor walked home. He passed some children playing on the steps and seemed to barely notice them as they marched up and down the steps.

"Do you think he has done it?" asked Inspector Best, watching Taylor disappear around the corner.

"I'm not sure. Something doesn't seem right."

"With what?"

"With him. His demeanour is all wrong. He has to know something."

Alexander Timpson turned towards the photo board. Adam Hamilton was listed as the victim, Gary Taylor was listed as one of five possible suspects, and Matt Fenton was listed as a possible target. Lines were drawn on the board which linked the people on there. Taylor had been drinking with Hamilton on the day that he was attacked and had discussed taking out Fenton. He had been to university with Fenton, but claimed he didn't know him. He had been in a relationship with La' Court, who had also been in a relationship with Fenton before she met Taylor and possibly afterwards as well. It said "current whereabouts unknown". They had no other information on La' Court.

Timpson was making a mental note of all the lines. They all pointed at Taylor—he had to be involved. Timpson was convinced that he was the cornerstone; it was just a question of joining the ends of the lines together. At the moment, it was all circumstantial. *Find the link and we find the motive. Find the motive and we have him*, thought Timpson. He looked at the board again—there had to be a line he was missing. It was a jigsaw with just one piece missing; get that and he would have the whole picture.

Timpson turned to Best. "What family does Taylor have?" he asked.

"None."

"None at all?"

"Taylor has never married and has never had children as far as we are aware. La' Court is his only girlfriend, and she left him years ago. He has not been in a relationship since,"

"What about other family?"

"His grandparents are all dead. He has no siblings. Both his parents were only children and both died young. Another thing, as a child he never had any pets—cat, dog, or rabbit—nothing at all to keep him company. And if Hamilton was a friend, he was the only one. He has no one to turn to."

Timpson stroked his chin. "No one at all. That makes him very dangerous. Do we know how his parents died?"

"I believe that they were both in an RTA."

"Do we know who the driver of the other vehicle was?"

"No, but I can check it out."

"You do that for me."

Best left the room. Timpson continued to study the picture of Taylor,

13

"What are you hiding from me?" he asked himself. He followed line after line but couldn't make that vital connection.

He already had one witness statement from the public house that said Taylor and Hamilton had discussed killing Fenton. The words she used were, "They said that they would blow his brains out."

She was not 100 per cent certain but thought that the threat had come from Taylor. She said that, as he left the public house, he put a pretend gun to his head as if to accentuate the point. She said Hamilton look scared. If it was Taylor that made the threat, then this could explain why he never mentioned it when they interviewed him.

Timpson was staring out of the window when Best returned. It was the middle of a heatwave; temperatures were at record levels. But the clouds were changing. A storm was coming—Timpson could feel it in his bones.

Timpson called his brother, Jonathan, who was a member of Fenton's cabinet. "We have a lead," he said.

"What kind of lead?"

"A loner with no friends and family, and he knows Fenton and La' Court."

"Do you have anything on him?"

"Not yet."

"Keep digging and keep me informed of your progress."

The minister hung up without even saying goodbye.

Best re-entered the room around twenty minutes later. She approached Timpson cautiously.

"Well?" he asked.

"The information about the car crash is in a sealed envelope."

Sealed envelope was the technical name for something that was confidential.

"And what does it say?"

"It says that I do not have the authority to access the information. It is above my pay scale."

Timpson turned to Best. "Why would a simple RTA from seven years ago be in a sealed envelope?"

Best shook her head.

Timpson looked at Taylor's photograph again. "He is or was a no-body.

His parents are nobodies. So who was in the other car, that's what we need to find out."

Best turned to go. "I know someone in archives. I will look into it and get back to you."

Daniel Hobson was sitting at his corner desk. He scowled at Timpson and Best as they spoke in hushed whispers. He was the third most senior officer there but always seemed to get overlooked for Meadows. He looked across at Meadows; she was busy typing away and smiling a self-confident smile of satisfaction. Hobson despised her and the attention that she got. It was no wonder he had applied for and received an invite to the Corporation's recruitment drive. Maybe they would treat him with the respect that he felt he deserved

Timpson had been planning Fenton's walkabout for several weeks. Everything had been going smoothly so far, better than he could have expected. Then this turned up on his doorstep—a serious assault on one of the fanatics that he had been tracking. He didn't need to get bogged down with a long investigation, so he had Inspector Best take charge of the assault on Adam Hamilton. He had every faith in her abilities and knew she would get a quick result,

He thumbed through the notes that they had got so far. They knew that Hamilton was going to do something when Fenton came to town— they had history and it wasn't good. The night of the attack, he had been drinking with Taylor. According to a witness statement, the conversation was a bit heated. They had just interviewed Taylor, and he had not mentioned this. Either the witness had misconstrued the conversation or Taylor was hiding something.

Hamilton had still not regained consciousness since the attack, and yet Taylor had never asked how he was. Timpson thought this was very strange. If he had been told that his only friend had been attacked after they had been drinking together the night before, the first thing he would do was ask if his friend was alright. Something was defiantly not right here.

Timpson scribbled some notes and observations in the file.

Timpson called the hospital. There was no change in Hamilton's condition—he was very weak but still alive. It would help them out enormously if he would come around.

Timpson's phone rang. It was one of Fenton's representatives that

15

worked with his brother, wanting to know how the preparations were going.

"Everything is on track at the moment, nothing to worry about."

But Timpson was worried his brother was checking up on him. The attack on Hamilton appeared to be random but had occurred at a most inopportune moment. It could upset everything. He needed to find out who was behind the attack on Hamilton and how this would affect Fenton's little walkabout. He had only a couple of days to go before the walkabout started, and he needed to be ready for it. If anyone was after Fenton, this was the time, and he needed to be on his toes. He couldn't let anything else get in the way. He could already feel the heat—if his brother was getting nervous then something was up. He already disagreed with Fenton doing the tour.

CHAPTER 4

THE CORPORATION

His alarm rang with a shrill chirping sound to signal the start of another new day. Gary Taylor stretched out his right arm and slapped his hand down hard on his alarm clock; the ringing stopped.

Gary got out of bed. The sun was shining brightly; in the distance he could hear a cock crow, signalling in the start of a new day.

Gary made some breakfast. He sat at the table looking at the letter, contemplating what he would do with his life. He had no job to go to; how would he fill in his days? Today was the day of the recruitment drive at the Corporation. He wondered if he should go. Then he thought, *Why not, I can see what they have to offer.*

Taylor washed and changed. He put on a clean shirt but didn't wear a tie. He got out his best shoes, which were still tight and rubbed on his heels. He put a plaster on his heel just to be on the safe side—he didn't want it to blister.

Gary Taylor took a slow leisurely walk to the Corporation.

He walked down Wellington Street where he passed a group of children playing in the street. As he went along, they were marching like soldiers and singing songs. He came to a T-junction—a ninety-degree turn to the right was Nelson Lane, which headed back towards town; straight on was Washington Road, which was a dead-end street. Only one building was on Washington Road; this was the Corporation. It was surrounded by a large brick wall.

Twenty yards down Washington Road was the entrance to the Corporation. It had a large gate which was two tall wooden doors painted in green. The paint was fading and, at places, peeling off. The doors were open in welcome for today's visitors.

Taylor nervously approached the doorway. Domenic Clarkson himself was there to greet the people who had turned up. He had worked with Gary Taylor for five years but hardly seemed to recognise him.

There were about twenty people there. Clarkson took them inside. They crossed a large cobbled courtyard and headed for a brick building at the back of the yard. Clarkson took them in through the main door where they were all given a visitor's pass. Clarkson then took them up some stairs that went off to the right; they reached the next level. He took them along a short corridor. To their left was a door; straight on, more stairs continued upwards. Clarkson stopped at the door and waited for everyone to catch up. Then he opened the door, which lead into an auditorium.

"Please take a seat," said Clarkson, the first words that he had spoken since Taylor had got there.

Gary Taylor walked in and found a seat in the sixth row. He moved along to the end of the row. Clarkson was at the front by the stage, talking to a man in a white coat. He looked around at the audience that had gathered.

The door to the auditorium opened up, and a girl walked, or more appropriately, staggered in. She was not a slim woman and wore a dress that was far too short. She made her way along the row in which Gary Taylor was sitting and seemed to be heading straight for him. Clarkson climbed the stairs on the far side as if he were trying to cut her off. She sat next to Gary Taylor.

"Hello, gorgeous," she said. "I'm Rose. What's your name?"

Clarkson climbed the last step—he now stood next to Taylor. "Rose, you don't need to be here." He turned to Taylor. "You don't need to get to know this one. She's trouble," he said.

Clarkson moved past Taylor and moved Rose on to the next seat. He sat between them.

They sat for a while as the auditorium filled up. The girl looked like she had been drinking. "I'm not a bad girl," she said. "Really, I'm not."

She seemed to be trying to direct the conversation to Taylor, but Clarkson shut her up. "Be quiet," he said, and he put his hand over her mouth.

She tried to bite his hand. He moved it away and told her to calm down.

A man in a white coat, looked like he could be a doctor, stood at the front of the auditorium and appealed for calm. Then he addressed them all.

"Before we start, I need half a dozen volunteers to take part in a little social experiment."

Gary never volunteered for anything after the issue with the magician. He just wished people would leave him alone. He hoped that they would take the girl that sat next to Clarkson. Another man in a white coat, who was slightly balding, came up the aisle and pointed at a man in the fourth row. "Will you come down to the front sir?" he asked.

Gary felt a sense of relief, but it was not to last long. The man in the white coat came down his row and tapped the girl on the shoulder. "Can you come down to the front please miss."

Gary started to sweat. He could feel the man's eyes burning through him. He stared at the man, willing him to go away. The man turned as if to go, then looked at the rows behind them and turned again to face Gary. "You, sir," he said, "would make a good candidate. Would you like to come down to the front?"

"How many people do you need?"

"Just six, and you are the sixth."

Reluctantly Gary stood up. Clarkson also stood up to let him through. "Good luck," he said.

Gary smiled nervously at him and followed the man to the front of the stage.

A door led into a small room. The girl was in the room making an almighty fuss. Another man in a white coat with horn-rimmed glasses had marked the back of her hands with a blue marker pen and told her to leave through a side door.

"Come in." He beckoned Gary into the room. "Hold your hands out in front of you with your palms facing downwards."

Gary did as he was told. The man in the white coat got the blue marker pen and put a blue dot on the back of both of his hands. "Now follow the young lady through that door." He pointed to Rose, who still stood in the doorway. Gary walked towards Rose. She went through the doorway; Gary followed her.

As he went through the doorway, he was covered in water. It felt like someone had deliberately sprayed him with a water gun. He looked around but could only see Rose. They were outside in a courtyard. It was dark. He looked up but could see no stars, only a darkness that seemed to surround them.

He followed Rose across the yard. At the far side was a grassy bank that went upwards. Rose walked aimlessly towards the bank; Gary followed her. Rose started to climb the bank. Gary looked up. He could see the silhouette of a man on the bank so he followed Rose. He climbed the bank. The other four volunteers were near the top.

As Gary climbed the bank, he could hear the children singing again—marching up a hill and marching down again. Gary stopped halfway up. He heard the children sing, "When he was halfway, he was neither up nor down." Gary looked around. He felt another spray of water. He looked at his hands—they seemed to be covered in blue ink.

Gary looked around at the other five. They were all expressionless. Then they started to walk down the bank again. Gary let them all walk past him. He tried to grab Rose's arm as she walked past, but he missed. He was stunned that he had missed her,

He heard a voice below telling them to come back in. Gary started to walk back in. He tried again to look up at the sky, but above him still was only blackness. He wondered if he really was outside or if this was just a room made to look like it was outside. At the bottom of the bank, the balding man in a white coat guided him back inside. The other man in a white coat was cleaning Rose's hands. The last of the other four men was just going back out into the auditorium.

Gary walked into the room. The second man in a white coat had just finished with Rose. She started to leave. The man asked Gary to hold his hands out. Gary did as he was told, but he was watching Rose leave through the door.

The man scraped the back of Gary's hand and pulled from nowhere a small cylinder about ten millimetres in length and two millimetres in diameter from the back of Gary's hand.

Gary could hear the children singing again, but this time he could hear two voices in the background talking. He couldn't hear what they were saying—he was straining to hear the voices over the sound of the children singing. He thought he heard one say, "He's not responding."

Gary looked at the men in white coats. They both wore a name badge, but he could not read the names on the badges—they were blurred. He looked at the first man. He wore heavy-set glasses, he could see that clear enough, but the name on his badge eluded him. Either this was deliberate or there was something wrong with his vision. He looked at the second man, who was balding. He could quite clearly see his features, but again, he could not read his name badge.

The first man in the white coat started to scrape his left hand. Then, quite suddenly, without warning, Gary flung his right arm out in front of him, pointing towards the wall as the man in the white coat pulled a second cylinder from his left hand. He moved his right arm, pointing outwards towards the door to the courtyard.

The children were still singing in his head. He bent his right arm at the elbow ninety degrees, so his arm went out to the right but was now again pointing at the wall in front of him.

Over the singing, he thought he heard one of the voices say, "Give it time."

The man now wiped his left hand with a damp cloth. Gary pulled his arm inwards so that his forearm went across his chest. He could feel himself doing this but had no control over it. He couldn't stop himself from doing it. He then brought his arm down by his side. The singing had stopped, but he could still hear voices in the background. One said, "He could be the one."

The second man in the white coat then wiped down his right hand. "That's it," he said. "You're done. You can go back into the auditorium."

The two men in the white coats smiled at him as he left. Gary went into the auditorium where a third man in a white coat with a goatee beard was thanking everyone for coming and said that they could now all go home. *Is that it?* Gary thought to himself. *Have I missed it all.*

He looked around the auditorium. People were getting up to leave. There was no sign of Clarkson anywhere. He noticed the clock on the wall—he had been there for over two hours, yet it only felt like five minutes. He wondered where all the time went. *What have I missed? Have I passed up the opportunity of being recruited whilst I was in that little room?*

21

What was that all about? He hadn't actually done anything and now it was all over. Gary saw Rose exiting through the door. He rushed after her, but by the time he reached the door there was a queue to get out, and she was gone.

CHAPTER 5

THE CITIZENS CHARTER

Matthew Fenton was two years older than Gary Taylor. They both went to the same university, although Gary didn't remember him from his time at university. They were studying different subjects, but Gary's then girlfriend, Vivianne La' Court, did study the same subject as Fenton. She did come across him several times, although this was only in her first year, as Fenton was then in his final year.

Back then, Fenton was not the politician he is now, and there was nothing about him to say that he would do much with his life. Back then, he was more interested in partying than party politics.

It was not until four years after he had finished at university that Fenton stood for the first time as a politician. He stood in a safe seat and won with a big majority. Only a year after winning his seat, he was promoted to the shadow cabinet, taking a small role in the shadow department for transport. After two years there, he was promoted to shadow treasury minister, and whilst there, he had the idea for the Citizens Charter. It bugged him that too many people claimed too much money for doing nothing, and he had a plan to change all that. At the annual conference, the leader of the party was taken ill, and Fenton was thrust into the job as leader of the opposition. It was not a job that he had wanted to do, but all the other candidates had issues that made them unpopular. The party had opted for a safe pair of hands.

Now Fenton had the platform that he needed, and things were about to change. His big idea was to get rid of all benefits, as he thought people were abusing the system and were not going out to work because they didn't have to. Some were getting more than others and were making multiple claims. Fenton's idea was that everyone would get the same whether they worked or not. This would be the Citizens Charter, and every man and woman over the age of twenty-one who had lived in the UK for more than five years would be paid £200 per week.

It was a bold move to try and bring this in and would have plenty of opposition particularly from those already claiming benefits, some would have the benefits reduced others would get money that they had never had before The way Fenton looked at it, everyone would get the same, so there would be no abusing the system. The money for the Citizens Charter would be paid for from the existing benefits scheme and would be propped up by the utilities companies. He decided that the utilities companies (gas, electric, and water companies) were charging far too much for the services that they offered and that they should be non-profit organisations—all their profits would be taken by the government to help pay for the Citizens Charter. He didn't want the companies over charging customer to make bigger and bigger profits putting people into poverty so any profits they made he would take away from them, his theory was that this would force them to lower their prices again it would benefit everyone.

The only way you would not get the payments was if you emigrated from the country or were sent to prison for a term of over one year. Then you would have to reapply one year after your return to the country or five years after your release from prison, and it would be down to the government to make the final decision as to whether or not to return the benefit to the applicant.

Fenton had the idea that if someone was working and they lost their job, they would continue to receive the £200 so they didn't need to claim unemployment benefit—they still got a decent amount to live on.

If someone was not working and they got a job, they didn't lose the money they were getting, so would still have a backup plan if their circumstances changed.

If a person had a disabled child, they would have the £200 to pay for the child's upkeep. If they had a partner, the partner also got the £200, so they would have £400 between them. If the child was over twenty-one then they would have £600 a week coming in, so there would be no need to claim any invalidity benefits. He assumed that this would be more than enough to care for someone and cover all the costs.

Immigration also featured highly on the Citizens Charter. He didn't want people coming in to the country just to claim the benefit they had to prove their worth to the country, he wanted a country that was sustainable and everyone got the same no matter where you were from or what your background was, he wanted to move the country on to make Britain Great again. If the immigrants didn't become British citizens within five years of entering the county, they would be forced to leave. To make their claim for the money, they had to be over twenty-one and had to have been a British citizen for at least five years. To become a British citizen, they now had to attend a citizenship ceremony and swear allegiance to the Queen and to the country. Anyone who had sworn allegiance to the country and commits acts of terror would be tried for treason, a crime against the Queen and the state.

Exiles—anyone who had left the country and not returned within a year—would lose their right to claim. Also, their claim would end if they had lived permanently outside the UK for five years whether they made return visits or not.

Anyone who was given a prison sentence of more than a year would lose the benefit and also their right to claim British citizenship and would be returned to their county of birth, he wanted more than anything for the people to respect each other.

It was a bold move to make and had as many critics as it had supporters. But the move had won his party their first general election in fifteen years, and now Fenton was the prime minister. He was hated by as many people as loved him. He was the most popular prime minister since Churchill and the most hated since Thatcher. He had made his mark—the Citizens Charter had divided opinion, and it had now been in force for three years. Most of the grumbling had now died down and people were getting used to the idea of having money for nothing.

Another of Fenton's ideas was to bring banks and shops back on to the high streets in order to bring people out into the open—he didn't want people hiding inside all day. He wanted an active nation that was alive and thriving, not a nation of keyboard warriors. He wanted a vibrant country, where the masses were out in the open and people could mingle. He wanted jobs for everyone.

If Fenton saw something that needed changing then he changed it. He didn't spend six months talking about it—he got it done, even if it meant treading on a few toes along the way. Fenton was a doer, but now his policies were getting a little stale. He had not had any new ideas for about a year, and not only the public but his party were getting restless. They wanted him to come up with another big idea, but he had run out of ideas and was living on past glories. The public needed him to do something; they needed to be inspired.

He decided that he needed to go out amongst the masses, put his views forward, and see their reactions first hand. He needed to see if he could take the public with him. He needed to show his party that the public were still on his side. The vultures were hovering—if he was going to fall, there were many queueing up to take his place. This was the most vulnerable he had been since he came to power and his rivals knew it. They were ready to pounce. Security would be a big issue.

Jonathan Timpson was the security minister in charge of home affairs. He was the brother of Alexander Timpson, the chief inspector who was put in charge of the security operation. Jonathan was a trusted man and would be made responsible for making sure that Fenton's walks around the country went ahead without a hitch. In his brother, Alexander Timpson, he had a trusted ally.

Alexander had been given twelve weeks to set up his team; now it was just three weeks till the tour started. Timpson had finally got his team in place. His first recruit was Leanne Best, who he had worked with at his previous station. Between them they had assembled a small team of twelve people.

They had been given an old disused station in Milton just north of Barnet. The only people that were currently in the station were Julie Gillien and Donald Megson, who ran the archives department in the basement. Here they kept old records that were often used to help with cold cases. They were important people who could find anything, but for years they were kept out of the way. Now they would have to share the building with Timpson and his team. Gillien had known Leanne Best for several years, she had known Leanne as a raw recruit when she first started, but Alexander Timpson and the rest of his team were strangers to her. Gillien felt that she would be able to put up with them if Megson could. She wasn't expecting them to cause too much trouble to her. After all, she was tucked away in the basement out of harm's way—for now anyway.

CHAPTER 6

UNUSUAL BEHAVIOUR

His alarm rang with a shrill chirping sound to signal the start of another new day. Gary Taylor stretched out his right arm. He grabbed the clock and threw it at the far wall. The clock hit the wall with a thud and broke into pieces. The alarm continued to ring, but now was more of a warble than a ring; it annoyed Gary more than the ringing alarm. He got out of bed and walked over to where the broken clock lay warbling. Today there was no sun beaming through the curtains. The day was overcast and there looked to be a threat of rain in the air.

Gary picked up the clock and slammed it against the wall. More bits fell to the floor, and the warbling sound of the broken alarm stopped at once. Gary could hear children singing about marching soldiers up a hill. This was now the fourth day that he had heard the song and it was getting to him.

Gary's hands started to itch. He looked down—he had two small scabs, one on the back of each hand. They looked like crucifixion marks, as if he'd had a nail hammered through each hand, and they were itching. He rubbed them but the itching didn't go away. He rubbed them again and again but the scabs still itched. He ran cold water from the tap over the back of his hands.

He went to the table where he had a cold cup of tea. He went back to the kitchen and put the kettle on. He could hear the children singing about marching. In the background, he thought he heard a voice say, "Give it time."

"Give what time?" he shouted out aloud to no one in particular.

Gary flung out his right hand in front of him. He knew what he was doing, but he couldn't stop himself from doing it. He put his arm out to the right.

He wanted to scream out again, but he couldn't say anything. He bent his arm at the elbow pointing out in front of him. Then he pulled his arm across his chest before dropping it by his side and the singing stopped. *Why am I doing this?* he thought.

The scabs on the back of his hand were itching again. Gary rubbed them and put some cream on them, then decided he would go and see his doctor. He rang for an appointment. Normally, he would be told it would take five days to see a doctor, but today they had a cancellation. He was asked if he could come down for half past nine. Gary didn't need to be asked twice; he was there for ten past.

Gary sat nervously in the waiting room. He was rubbing the back of his hands.

He tried to read the notices on the walls. He was having trouble with his concentration, and he was fidgeting. He looked around—there was only one other person in front of him and another two had come in behind him. He scratched at the scabs on the back of his hands. He smiled a nervous smile at the old woman watching him scratch his hands, then he turned his gaze away from her. He looked up at the clock on the wall; it had just turned twenty-five past nine. He tapped his feet on the ground. The old woman glared at him so he stopped immediately. The clock had moved on another minute. The time dragged by real slow. He looked again at the clock—it had barely moved since he last looked.

His name was called out, and he went in to see Dr Swanson.

The doctor was an old-ish man in his early sixties. What little hair he had left was turning grey. He wore thick glasses. Gary assumed that he would be about the same age as his father. The doctor beckoned him to sit down.

"What can I do for you today?" the doctor asked.

Gary sat as he had been asked to do, then held out his hands.

"Can you look at the scabs on the backs of my hands please?"

The doctor looked puzzled. "There are no marks on your hands."

"Just there," said Gary as he started to rub the back of his hand again.

"I see no marks on your hands."

"Take a look please."

The doctor took hold of Gary's right hand. He could see no mark. He rubbed his thumb over the spot that Gary had pointed to and he could feel nothing at all.

He then did the same with Gary's left hand. Again, he could see nothing and he could feel nothing.

"Is there anything else troubling you?" the doctor asked.

"I keep pulling my arm up for no reason at all and pulling it across my chest before letting it drop down to my side."

"Why do you do this?"

"I don't know it's an uncontrollable urge to do it. I can feel myself doing it, but I cannot stop it."

The doctor was scribbling down a few notes. "Do you know of anything that could trigger this reaction?"

"I keep hearing a song in my head, the same song over and over, and every time I hear this song, I do this funny action that I cannot stop."

"What is this song?"

"It's something about a duke marching his soldiers up a hill and down again."

"That's not a song."

"Yes, it is. I hear it every day."

"It's not a song. It is a children's nursery rhyme, something that parents teach to very young children. And they do a marching action to go with it, pulling up the arms and swinging them across the chest, very much like what you have described to me. Have you had any trauma recently?"

"I've just lost my job last week."

The doctor was still scribbling down notes. "I think this is a repressed memory from your youth which has been brought out by the trauma of you losing your job. You will get over it in a day or two."

The doctor wrote out a prescription for some tablets.

"What are these for?"

"They're to stop your anxiety. If you feel that you cannot control your actions, take one of these and it will calm you down."

Gary was not convinced, but he thanked the doctor for his time, he shook his hand, and started out for home.

Gary went out on to the street; it was now raining and there was no one about. He took the shortest route home. Down by the canal, he could hear the children singing. He stopped and looked around; there was no one about. He let his body do the action with the arms. When he had finished, he looked around again just to check that no one was watching him do these funny little actions. "Repressed memory indeed," he called out aloud before continuing home.

He was soaked through when he got home. He hung his coat up and went into the kitchen to put the kettle on. He put his hand out to reach for the kettle, then he flung his arm out to the right. He could hear the singing again and voices in his head chattering behind the singing. He could not hear what they were saying. He looked out of the kitchen window—the rain continued to fall and nothing was moving outside.

There were no children marching, no people walking, and no cars driving. Everything was quiet. Gary Taylor made a cup of tea. He sat at the table with his head in his hands, wondering what to do. He scratched the back of his hands—they were itching again. He put the radio on. The big discussion was about Fenton's tour. He changed channels, and they were playing that damn song about the duke. He reached for the radio, and he heard a voice in his head ask, "Is he ours?"

"No, I'm not yours," he shouted at the radio. "I will never be yours."

Gary Taylor switched the radio off and sat back to drink his tea. His eyes were getting tired; they started to close. He drifted into a deep sleep. He was standing in a line surrounded by soldiers. They were waiting for the order to go. The Duke rode past on his horse—he looked like the Duke of Wellington in all his finery. The soldiers looked like the tin soldiers that he played with as a child, all in their scarlet red uniforms. He heard a cry: "Onwards!" The soldiers started marching. In front was a very steep hill that climbed has high as he could see. He was marching up the hill. He heard a voice say, "We have to keep going, right on to the end."

Taylor looked around—there was no one with him; he was all alone. He was standing at the top of a hill. There was a cool mist surrounding the top of the hill and no sign of the other soldiers. He knew that he needed to go down again.

CHAPTER 7

IT'S HAPPENING AGAIN

His alarm rang with a shrill chirping sound to signal the start of another new day. Gary Taylor stretched out his right arm and slapped his hand down hard on his alarm clock. There was no clock there, and yet he still heard it ringing.

Gary Taylor got up, had his breakfast, and then went out to fetch the morning paper.

The rains had stopped, but still, the ground was wet. Gary Taylor seemed to be oblivious of everything that was going on around him. He didn't notice anyone in the street, yet Domenic Clarkson walked right across his path—he didn't notice he was there. He bought the paper and walked home again without even looking up at his surroundings. Gary Taylor was in a state of confusion. He didn't know what was happening to him. Every time he heard the children sing that song, he would start to throw his arms about. He knew he was doing it but couldn't stop it from happening.

Gary Taylor was sitting in his room reading the paper. Matthew Fenton's tour of the country had been put back a week due to an attack on the chancellor, Luke Appleyard. He was out and about, doing a sort of practice run for Fenton to judge the public feeling. He had been about to meet a few people when someone had come up to him and poured a packet of flour over his head. Fenton was worried about security, as this was the second such attack on a politician in two days.

After the attack on Appleyard, Fenton had sent a strongly worded letter to the head of security. Timpson had replied that he hadn't put the security in place for Appleyard and there would be a bigger police presence for his own tour, which seemed to pacify Fenton.

Timpson knew that something was wrong and that Fenton had been targeted, but he couldn't let Fenton know this. The tour had to go ahead as planned, and he needed to be sure that he was ready for it. He had suspicions of who could be involved, but without any hard evidence, he couldn't do anything.

Timpson called Best into his office. He needed to go over the plans with her again just to be on the safe side. He needed to know if she had got anything else on Taylor, his number one suspect, but they were having issues tracking his movements.

Gary Taylor laughed at the picture of Appleyard covered in flour. Then he stopped laughing. He saw the picture of the attacker who had been arrested at the scene. He didn't know the guy but recognised the face. He had seen him at the Corporation—he was one of the six who had been volunteered to go outside. He had seen him close up when they were on the hill. There was no mistake—it was the same man.

Gary Taylor was agitated; he knew something was wrong. He was pacing his room. He could hear the children singing again then he threw his right arm out in front of him. He knew what he was doing—it was the little marching movement—but he didn't know why he was doing it. And he couldn't stop himself from doing it. He pushed his arm out to the right, then bent it at the elbow so that he was pointing forward again, then pulled his arm across his chest. He could hear the children singing, and in the background, he thought he heard a voice say, "Give it time."

Gary pulled his arm back down beside his side and the singing stopped.

He felt the scabs at the back of his hands itching, and he rubbed them again.

Gary looked at the box of tablets that the doctor had prescribed for him and put them down again. Something was happening. He didn't know what was happening, but he did know that the tablets were not the answer.

Gary looked at the newspaper, at the headline which said that Matthew Fenton had delayed the start of his tour of the country again by another week after the latest attack on a member of his cabinet.

He got up and walked over to the window. He looked out of the window; all was quiet and still. Nothing was moving outside when all at once there was a group of children marching up the road. He couldn't hear them, but he knew that they were singing that song. They were marching down the road led by a teacher encouraging them to sing the song.

Gary Taylor put his arm out in front of himself, then out to his right-hand side before bending it at the elbow. It was happening again and he couldn't stop it. He pulled his arm across his chest, then he dropped it down by his side. He looked out of the window and the children had gone. They had marched up the hill, but he knew that they would march down again. He scratched at the scab on his hands—something was happening to him and he couldn't stop it. It felt like he was being controlled like a puppet on a string. The scab on his hands itched—was this where the strings went in? Why could the doctor not see them; was he blind, or just pretending? Was the doctor a part of the master plan?

Gary made himself a cup of tea. He sat at his dining table staring at the fire. He refused to move from his spot. He stayed sitting in the same spot for six hours. Why him? What was so special about him? As far as Gary could see, he was a nobody with no job, no wife, no family, nothing to tie him down, nobody who would miss him if he wasn't there.

Was that it? Was it because he had no ties? Did this make him expendable?

Gary could hear the children singing. He wanted to cry, but all he could do was to fling out his arm and do the funny little movement. Three hours later, it started all over again—first the singing, then the arm movements. Gary Taylor went to bed but he could not sleep. He could hear voices in his head. One voice kept asking the same question: "Do we have him?"

The second voice always replied, "Give it time."

Then, as he lay in bed, he could hear the children singing.

His dreams were disturbing too. He was dressed in a military uniform, marching up a hill with a rifle strapped across his shoulder.

Next to him was a girl. He recognised the face but couldn't think from where. She stumbled and fell to the ground. He stopped and helped her up. "We have to keep going," he told her

---

Gary Taylor didn't need an alarm clock to wake him in the morning—he had struggled to sleep most of the night. When he did sleep, his dreams troubled him. He was up early and washed by 5 a.m. He was in the bathroom looking in the mirror when the singing started again. He watched himself in the mirror as he flung out his arm out, but he didn't recognise the reflection in the mirror. It was him but it wasn't him. It was like he was watching someone else in his body. He dropped his arm to his side and the singing stopped.

Gary Taylor had an uncontrollable urge to cry. The tears rolled down his cheeks. He knew something was wrong, but he had no idea what to do to sort it out. "Sitting here crying will not get things sorted," he said to himself as he wiped his eyes dry.

He thought about what the doctor had said, that it was a repressed memory and losing his job had been the trigger. He looked at the bottle of tablets. He held the little bottle tightly in his hands. He looked at the label, but all the words were blurred. He couldn't read what the medication he was about to take was. Like the name badges at the Corporation, he could see everything clearly apart for the written words. He knew the doctor was wrong; he knew the tablets were not the answer, and he put the bottle down again, still unopened. This had something to do with his visit to the Corporation. He had been there for over two hours but could only remember five minutes. Something had happened to him; he needed to find out what had happened in those two hours.

This was not going to stop until he got some answers. Domenic Clarkson would know what was going on. He decided that he needed to see Domenic. He decided that he would go to the Corporation, and he would ask Domenic what they had done to him. Domenic was a friend, or he had been a friend. He had to tell him what was going on. He decided that he would go down to the Corporation as soon as it got light, or maybe after nine—he was not sure what time they opened. *Nine will do*, he thought as he put the kettle on again.

CHAPTER 8

GILLIEN

Inspector Best needed to find out what was in the sealed envelope—this could be the clue to breaking the case. Wayne Taylor was just a doctor and his wife, Martha, was a receptionist, so why would their deaths be such a mystery? After all, it was just an ordinary RTA.

Inspector Leanne Best had served in the force for many years and had plenty of contacts. She decided to call her friend Julie Gillien, who worked as a filing clerk in the criminal records department in the basement of the building Best was now stationed at. If anyone knew how to get into a sealed envelope, she would be the one.

Inspector Best picked up the phone, then looked around the office. She then put down the phone and decided that she would see Gillien face to face.

Timpson was on the phone in his office. No one noticed as she slipped out and went down to the basement where the criminal records were stored.

Julie Gillien had just turned forty, but she looked older. She had never married; she was dedicated to her work. If someone commented that she was only a filing clerk, she would reply that she was the best at doing her job.

She had been with the force for around twenty years with most of it in criminal records as a filing clerk. For the last seven years, she had been the chief archivist and carried top-level security status. She knew everything about everything; if anything was required, then Gillien was your go-to person. She loved to get to the bottom of a mystery and was an ace at finding facts and joining the dots. Inspector Best had used her before on cases, and Gillien had brought her some invaluable help.

Inspector Best had never been down in the basement before. Previously, Best had been at Harrington station and had always called Gillien on the phone. There was no elevator, and she had to go down the stairs all the way to the basement. There were no windows down there, and for Best, it felt gloomy, spooky even—the ghosts of past cases could live down here, and Gillien sat amongst them.

Julie Gillien looked up in surprise. She didn't often get visitors down here, and this was the first time that Leanne Best had come to see her.

"What can I do for you, Leanne?" she asked.

"I'm working on a case. I need information on a suspect's parents that were killed in an RTA, but their information is in a sealed envelope."

"Then why have you come to see me?"

"I thought you may be able to unseal it so that I could take a peak."

"The envelopes are sealed for a reason you know."

"It could be important to the case that I'm working on. I've hit a brick wall and need a little break."

"What are you looking for?"

Inspector Best sat down at the desk opposite to Gillien and leaned forward. "It is just a doctor and his wife, Wayne and Martha Taylor. They were killed in an RTA about six or seven years ago. We need to know the name of the driver of the other vehicle."

"Was this doctor an important person?"

"Not as far as we can tell, and his wife was just a receptionist."

Gillien shook her head. "If the doctor and his wife were unimportant then the person driving the other vehicle must have been someone of importance, as only high officials have the privilege to seal the envelopes. You need to be careful—you could be stepping on someone's toes here."

"Can you do it for me?"

"I'll have a look into it for you. But you cannot tell anyone you are looking into this, not even Timpson. Don't ring me about this. Come down here again tomorrow, and I'll see what I've got."

Best got up to leave. "Thank you, Julie," she said. "You're a star."

"Thank me tomorrow—if I have anything for you. I'm on my own today. Megson has gone down with that bug that is going around, so it may take longer than usual. I'll let you know when I've got something."

Inspector Best returned to her office. Timpson was still on the phone in his office, and everyone else was just doing what they should be doing. No one looked up as she returned. She sat at her desk as if she had not been away.

In the corner, Daniel Hobson was making mental notes; Best had been away for twenty minutes.

Gillien had a password decoder, which no one was supposed to know about, and she could use it to get into the sealed envelope. It wasn't straightforward—she had to type in the keywords and needed the date the envelope was sealed. She knew the date of the reported deaths so put that in as the start date and did a search for up to a week after that date. A message on her screen read: *searching for data, this will take a little while, please wait.*

She sat and waited … and waited. The system was still searching. Gillien went out and got a coffee. When she came back, the system was still searching. Gillien sat down and took a sip of coffee; the system was still searching.

Eventually the screen changed and a new message popped up: *password found, press enter to view the password.*

Gillien pressed enter, noted the password, and went to open the sealed letter. The system asked her to enter her rank and confirm her security access. She had high-level security access because at times she had to legally open sealed envelopes, and she needed the access to do so. Once this was confirmed, the system asked her to re-enter the password. She entered the password, and the screen said: *witness protection.* Her eyes bulged as she read the information.

Taylor's parents were not dead; they had been given new identities. *Why?* she wondered.

Suddenly a warning light started to flash, a message read: *illegal entry detected.* Someone knew that she had broken the seal on the envelope. "Sugar," she cursed. She knew that now she would be in trouble. Whoever had sealed the envelope would be coming for her or Leanne—or both. She needed to see Leanne. She needed to warn her that they had been found checking the sealed envelope.

But first she needed to reseal the envelope. Gillien sealed the envelope and reset a new password as *not dead*. She wrote the password on a notepad, *not dead*. She looked at the written password. "Too obvious," she said to herself.

She wrote over the password again, pressing down hard on the paper, then tore the note from the pad. She felt the remaining page; she could feel the outlines of the words. "That will do."

Gillien shredded the original note then went upstairs to see if she could find Leanne Best.

The room was empty apart from Lisa Barber, Glen Morris, and Danny Hobson.

She asked Lisa If she knew where Leanne Best was.

"She's gone out with Meadows, gone to see some bloke—I think he's called Tyler."

"Could it be Taylor?"

"Yeah, that sounds about right."

Gillien thanked Lisa for the information and went outside.

Hobson was taking notes: *Best out with Meadows; Gillien looking for Best.*

Gillien went outside. She went down the steps and noticed a sinister looking man heading straight for her. She turned to go the other way, and there was another man coming for her from the opposite direction. Now she was in trouble.

Gillien turned to go back inside; there was another man coming down the steps holding out his warrant card in front of him.

"Miss Gillien, we need to talk," he said. "It's a matter of national security."

Gillien knew she was in trouble the moment the security message popped up, and Milton was only ten miles from the centre of London, but even so, she had not expected them to get there that fast. It had been only six minutes since the message flashed up, or were they already here watching her—or Leanne. She wondered if she had put her friend in danger, and if Leanne would find her message.

Two of the men grabbed Gillien by the arms and marched her around the corner, where the third man put a hood over her head and bundled her into a car, which drove off at speed. She heard one of the men tell the driver to slow down—they didn't need to be stopped.

Twenty minutes later, the hood was removed from her head, and she was standing in front of Wayne Taylor. Her suspicions were confirmed—Wayne Taylor was not dead for here he was, large as life, standing before her.

CHAPTER 9

GOING BACK

Gary could hear the sound of laughter. He could see Vivianne—she stood naked in front of him. She put her arms around him and kissed him. Gary had missed this. It felt so right, it felt so wrong. Vivianne stared into his eyes. Where had she been all this time? He had been longing for this. He held her close to him.

He could hear a voice in his head say "Is he ours?"

Gary looked at Vivianne—it wasn't Vivianne who lay by his side; it was the girl Rose from the Corporation.

"Nooooo!" he screamed.

Gary sat up in bed, beads of sweat rolling down his forehead. He had been dreaming. He looked for his clock; it was not there. The room was still dark, but he could not sleep.

He got up and went to the kitchen, put on the light, then boiled the kettle. The clock said it was four in the morning. His head hurt; the light hurt his eyes. His ears were ringing with the sound of children singing. His arms ached from the jerky marching movements. He wanted to scream but could make no sound.

Gary had never been up at this time before. He was unsure what to do, so he made a cup of tea and ate a slice of some toast, then he sat down at the table staring at the walls for over two hours.

Something was happening to him, but he couldn't work out what it was. It had all started when he went to the Corporation. He tried to think about what had happened. He remembered sitting in the auditorium, then standing on a hill and getting wet, but he remembered little else, only that he had met this girl there. He needed to go back; he needed to go back now. He looked at the clock—he needed to go back in five hours. For now, he needed another cup of tea more than anything else.

———◆◆✕◆◆———

Gary Taylor walked down Wellington Street. He reached the junction with Nelson Lane and Washington Road. He could see the Corporation in front of him. The big green doors were closed. He stood for a moment to compose himself, then he thought; *that's it, I'm going in.*

He marched purposely forward, but when he looked up, he was already halfway down Nelson Lane. He didn't want to come this way; he wanted to go down Washington Road. He wanted to turn around but kept walking on. He reached a café. The girl, Rose, was sitting outside at a table with her head in her hands. It looked like she had been crying. Gary didn't say anything. He wanted to go back to the Corporation; he needed to have a word with Domenic Clarkson. He needed to know what had happened at the Corporation. He remembered nothing of that day, only that he had met the girl sitting in front of him at the café and that they had stood on a hill in the rain, and he had met a man in a white coat—all the rest was a complete blank.

Gary turned around to go back to the Corporation. He arrived at his front door ten minutes later. He felt confused. He went inside and put the kettle on. *What happened today?* He wondered. The singing was in his head again. He held his right arm out in front of him, put it out to his right, bent it at the elbow, then he pulled his arm across his chest before dropping it down by his side again. He thought he heard a voice behind the singing say, "Do we have him?"

He didn't know who the voice was but imagined it to be one of the men in the white coats. He thought they were talking about him and realised then that he was not supposed to be hearing what they were saying.

The singing stopped, and he was back to normal. He went out and bought a newspaper.

The newspaper said that a politician had been attacked for the second time in three days. There was a picture of Steve Harrison covered in flour that had been thrown on him.

But the caption of the picture actually read that it was Luke Appleyard who was the victim. They had put in the right photograph but had associated it with the wrong politician. The article went on to say that, although the attacks were the same, there was nothing to connect the two attackers. Gary recognised the first attacker from the Corporation. The second attacker was the girl, Rose. They had nothing to connect the attackers, but Gary did.

It was time to go back and have a look at the Corporation. For a second time, Gary went down Wellington Street. He had his target in front of him, and he was going in. He looked up and again he was standing in front of the café on Nelson Lane. He didn't want to be here, but he couldn't turn back. The girl was again sitting at a table with her head in her hands.

Gary sat in front of her. "Hello," he said.

Rose looked up and said nothing. "I met you at the Corporation," he told her.

"What's that?"

"We went for an interview last week."

"Did we?"

"Don't you remember?"

"No, I've never seen you before."

"My name is Gary Taylor."

"I'm Rose."

"Yes, I know."

"How do you know?"

"We met last week."

"Really? You'd think I would remember that."

It was becoming a difficult conversation. Gary couldn't take anymore, so he decided to go home. He thanked Rose for talking to him and left. He took a slow walk down by the canal.

As he reached his front door, he could hear the children singing again. He wanted to put his key in the lock but, instead, held his arm out in front of him before putting it out to the right and then bending his arm at the elbow. Again, he could hear the two men talking in the background. The only sentence that he heard was one of them saying, "He's trying to resist us."

Gary pulled his arm across his chest, then he dropped it down by his side. Then the singing stopped. He put the key in the lock, opened the door. Then he took a look around the street to see if anyone was watching him.

The street was empty. He went inside. He was trembling, and his scabs on his wrists were itching. He tried to rub them but it did not help. He looked at the tablets that the doctor had prescribed him, picked up the container, and threw it at the wall.

◆━━━◆━✕━◆━━━◆

Gary went back again the following day. He reached the junction and stopped. He could see the green doors of the Corporation standing bold like sentries—no one shall pass.

He was going in. He set off at a brisk pace and headed towards the gates, but found himself standing outside the café on Nelson Lane again. The girl, Rose, was there again.

He didn't approach her right away. He stood by the kerb and watched Rose. She did nothing; she just sat there with her head in her hands. It looked like she was crying, but he couldn't be sure. He felt that she was waiting for someone. He watched her for ten minutes before he approached her.

"Hello," he said.

The girl looked up. "Do I know you?"

"I'm Gary."

"I'm Rose."

"Yes, I know."

"How do you know?"

"We spoke yesterday."

"Did we?"

"We talked about the Corporation."

"What's that?"

"It's the place where we first met."

"When?"

"Last week."

"Really? You'd think I would remember that."

Gary had a feeling of déjà vu. He had already had this conversation once, and she remembered nothing about it. Gary went home again.

Gary had tried to tell her about the Corporation and going into the

44

little room, but Rose just stared through him. She remembered none of it. She didn't even remember meeting him there yesterday. Gary talked to Rose for over an hour before he went home. He couldn't work out what was happening and why she could not remember him.

"There has to be some way to make her remember," he said to himself.

Gary Taylor went back to the café. The girl, Rose, was not there. In her place sat a tall blonde woman. He did not know her but felt that he had seen her before somewhere. He couldn't remember where.

Gary approached the blonde woman. "Where's Rose?" he asked.

"Who?"

"The girl who usually sits here."

"I'm sorry but I have no idea who you are talking about."

The woman put a £10 banknote on the table, walked across the road, got into a car, and drove off. As she departed, he remembered he had seen her that night he had been out with Tinky. She was the woman reading the paper in the back of the pub. She had to know something and now she was gone. He had no idea who she was or where to find her. He realised that he had just let a big opportunity slip by.

"What is happening!" he called out to no one in particular. He looked up to the sky, seeking inspiration that was not coming his way. He walked home again.

CHAPTER 10

A VISIT FROM THE LAW

Inspector Best was sitting at her desk filling in her time sheet when her phone rang. She was expecting a call from Gillien, so she picked up on the first ring. It wasn't Gillien; it was the hospital. They informed her that Adam Hamilton had passed away during the night without ever regaining consciousness. Leanne took down the notes. She now needed to go and see Taylor again.

The attack on Tinky Twinkletoes had now become a murder enquiry. Inspector Best went to see Timpson. He was on the phone in his office. She knocked on the door and entered.

He asked the caller to hold for a minute and put the phone down.

"Is this important?" he asked.

"Adam Hamilton passed away during the night. I'm going to see Taylor again."

"Take Meadows with you, don't see him alone. He could be dangerous."

Leanne Best asked Holly Meadows if she would come with her to see Taylor. As she got up, Daniel Hobson gave her a sideways glance as if saying "overlooked again". This was now starting to get to him, that he was always left inside. He scribbled another note on his pad.

Holly Meadows drove them to Gary Taylor's house. It was not far from the station, only a ten-minute walk. In the car, it took about three minutes to get there.

Gary Taylor was standing in his bathroom staring at the mirror. His arm was stretched out to the right, bent at the elbow, the sound of children singing in his head, when the doorbell rang. *Not now*, he thought.

He pulled his arm across his chest and the bell rang again. He pulled his arm down by his side. The singing stopped, but the scars on his wrists were itching. He wanted to rub them, but his doorbell rang again. He rushed down to the door and opened it. Inspector Best and WPC Meadows were standing at the door.

"May we come in?" asked Inspector Best.

Gary Taylor beckoned them in and led them to his living room. "Take a seat," he said, inviting them to sit down. "What can I do for you today?"

"Adam Hamilton passed away last night without regaining consciousness."

"How sad. He was a nice man. Can I get you a drink or something?"

"No thank you. We've come to tell you that this is now a murder enquiry, and we want to know about your movements on that night."

"I already told you this at the station."

"Why did you go by the old canal towpath that night?"

"It's the quickest way home. I often go that way."

"You weren't there waiting for Hamilton to come out then?"

"No, I went straight home."

"Any witnesses?" Meadows chipped in.

"Not unless someone was stalking me."

Inspector Best looked at WPC Meadows, then turned back to face Gary Taylor. "I don't think you grasp the gravity of your situation. Hamilton has died, and you are the number one suspect. You were the last to see him alive, and you haven't adequately accounted for your movements on the night of the attack. You can continue to play games with us, or we can take you down to the station. The choice is yours."

"I don't get it. Why are you hassling me? He was my friend. Why would I want to hurt him?"

"Do you know who else would want to hurt Hamilton?"

"No, I didn't really know him that well."

"I thought you said he was your friend." Meadow's butted in.

"Well, he is the nearest I have to a friend, but I still didn't know him that well. He was more of a friend of Vivianne's than mine."

"Where is Vivianne these days?"

"I have no idea. I've not seen her for about seven years. She has not tried to contact me since she left."

"Why did she leave?"

Gary Taylor shrugged his shoulders. "Time to move on I suppose."

WPC Meadows was looking around the room, then she spoke. "You have no photographs of your parents."

"No, I don't."

"Why is that?"

"It's because I have never had a picture of them to put up."

Meadows turned to Best. "Don't you think that's odd?"

Inspector Best approached Taylor. "Tell us about your parents," she asked.

"What do you want to know?"

"Who killed them?"

"They died in a car crash."

"Who was the driver of the other vehicle?"

"I don't know some random guy that had too much to drink ran a red light."

"If he was a random guy, why is the case file sealed. Access to the file is above my pay grade, and I have top-level security."

Gary Taylor was confused by what he had just heard. His head was spinning, he could hear children's voices singing again. This was now happening all too often and at the most inappropriate times. "If you'll excuse me, I have to go to the bathroom."

Gary Taylor rushed out to the bathroom. He had barely closed the door when he pushed out his right arm in front of him. *Why now?* he thought. The singing was the clearest he had heard it, and he thrust out his arm to his right then bent it at the elbow. He then put out his left arm. He pulled his right arm across his chest, then he put his left arm out to the left. He heard the voices again: "Do we have him?"

The second voice replied, "He will obey."

He bent his left arm at the elbow, then he dropped his right arm down by his side.

He heard WPC Meadows call out, "Are you OK, Mr Taylor."

He then pulled his left arm across his chest before dropping it down by his side. This was the first time that he had done the movement with both arms. He looked in the mirror—he was sweating. He ran water into the sink and rinsed his face. *They cannot see this*, he thought. *I need to get them out of here. This is happening more and more often. I need to go back to the Corporation and find out what they have done to me.*

He was staring at his reflection in the mirror. He didn't recognise himself—it was like he was watching someone else. He could see his father in the mirror. Taylor could feel the blood draining from his face as he stared at the picture of his father in the mirror. He rinsed his face again and looked back in the mirror—he was looking at himself again, but now he was trembling. He had gone cold and shivery.

WPC Meadows called out again. "Are you OK, Mr Taylor?"

"Just a minute," he replied. He knew he had to hold himself together whilst they were here. He couldn't afford to have another attack.

Taylor came out of the bathroom and made a pot of tea. They sat around his table. Best asked most of the questions, and it went on for about an hour. Taylor could hear the sound of children singing again.

All of a sudden, Meadows stood up and said, "That will be all, thank you for helping us with our enquiries, Mr Taylor."

Best shot her a sideways glance then also stood up. "Thank you, Mr Taylor, you have been most helpful."

They went outside; the door closed behind them.

Out of sight, Taylor was already flinging his arms out to the tune of the children. In his mind he was marching up the hill.

Outside, Meadows leaned back against the door. Inspector Best looked at her colleague—the colour had drained from her face. "Are you alright, Holly?" she asked, concerned about her friend.

WPC Holly Meadows was trembling. "Did you not feel it?" she asked.

"Feel what?"

Meadows shook her head. "I don't know how to explain it."

"Well, try then."

"Not here," she replied and walked unsteadily to the car.

Inspector Best opened the passenger door, and as WPC Holly Meadows climbed in, she took a glance back at the house. She thought she saw a curtain twitch, but couldn't be sure. She thought that Taylor was watching them, waiting for them to leave. In the car, Holly looked unwell. Her face had become ashen—she looked really ill.

Inspector Best drove them back to the station. Meadows didn't say a word on the way back. She stared out of the window at the darkening sky.

Holly Meadows needed to tell Leanne what she felt in Taylor's house, but she couldn't adequately describe what she felt. "Can we do this later?" she asked.

Holly had got some of her colour back, but still didn't look well. As they talked back at the station, Daniel Hobson watched and bit his bottom lip—he felt that they were deliberately keeping him out of the loop.

CHAPTER 11

GOING NOWHERE

The magician was standing in front of him. All around them was darkness. He couldn't see anyone else but the magician. He had two solid rings in his hands and tapped them together to prove that they were solid—they gave out a metallic chink. Gary had seen this before and was not impressed. The magician dropped the first ring, and they were joined together in a link like a chain. Gary could not hear anyone clapping. In fact, Gary could hear nothing at all. He seemed to be here on his own facing his biggest fear.

The magician said, "May I now introduce you to may assistant, Miss Magica."

Out of the shadows stepped Vivianne La' Court. She wore a sparkly skirt which was cut far too low at the front. She glided on to the stage holding her arms up in the air, milking the applause that was not there. Gary Taylor sat staring at Vivianne. *This cannot be happening*, he thought. She smiled right at him; it was a sweet smile, a sickly smile, not like Vivianne at all. She fluttered her eyes at him, willing him to come to her. He awoke with a start—he had been dreaming again. *They have put something in my head*, he reasoned with himself. I have to go back to the Corporation to sort this out. I have to find out what is happening to me.

Gary Taylor went back to sleep, but his dreams were troubled. He dreamed of the magician. He dreamed of Vivianne—he longed to see her again; he longed to hold her again. He had not seen her for seven years, and the longer he went without seeing her, the more he wanted her. He was once told, "You don't know what you've got until you lose it." That saying meant more to him now than ever before. He called her name, but this was not the Vivianne that he had spent many years with, and he knew it. Vivianne was gone and she was not coming back. He still wanted her and reached out for her. She melted away into the distance. In her place, he could see children marching up a hill, singing that damn song.

The children marched up the hill, then they marched down again. At the bottom of the hill they turned around to march back up, but this time he was now in their ranks, and he was in full military uniform. With a rifle across his shoulder, marching in rank and file, they were heading back to the hill. To his right was the girl, Rose. She smiled at him. They started to march up the hill. Halfway, he stumbled and fell to his knees. It felt so real he could feel the pain as his outstretched arms took the impact of the fall. He looked up and watched the others marching past him, relentlessly climbing the hill, forever going onwards and upwards not stopping for a moment. Someone grabbed his arm. He heard a female voice say to him, "We have to go on."

He looked up—it wasn't Rose. It was the policewoman that had been to his house. What was she doing here, and why was she marching up the hill? He hadn't seen her at the Corporation, this was nothing to do with her. *Why is she in my dream?*

He looked around; the soldiers were melting into a soft mist. He heard a male voice in his head say, "Do we have him?"

There was no reply. The voices in his head faded to nothing, and he drifted into a deep sleep.

❖◆✕◆❖

Gary Taylor awoke with a ringing in his head. He looked around; he still did not have an alarm clock, but he could hear it ringing. Gary Taylor desperately needed to go back to the Corporation. He was up and dressed early and out at the crack of dawn. This was probably too early.

He walked down to the canal. He stared for a moment into the murky waters, he decided that it was too early. He went home and had some breakfast before setting out again.

Just after nine in the morning, he marched down Wellington Street with a purposeful stride. He looked up, and again he was standing outside the café on Nelson Lane. Rose sat at a table with her head in her hands. He looked around—no one else was about. This is not where he wanted to be.

He turned around and walked down Nelson Lane. When he looked up he was down by the side of the canal where he had been just a couple of hours earlier in the day. He had no idea how he had got here. This, again, was not where he wanted to be.

Taylor went home. He sat at home for two hours then he went out. He walked down Wellington Street and found himself, again, outside the café on Nelson Lane. Rose was again sitting at a table. He cautiously approached her—he needed to get some answers.

She was always there; she had to know more than what she was letting on.

Gary sat in front of her. "Hello," he said.

Rose looked up and said nothing. "I met you at the Corporation," he told her.

"What's that?"

"We went for an interview last week."

"Did we?"

"Don't you remember?"

"No, I've never seen you before."

"My name is Gary Taylor."

"I'm Rose."

"Yes, I know."

"How do you know?"

"We met last week."

"Really? You'd think I would remember that."

How many more times am I going to have this same conversation with Rose, he thought. *There has to be some way to break the cycle.*

Gary was getting nowhere with Rose. He went home again.

He put on the radio; a report said that Matt Fenton's tour would start tomorrow. They then went on to interview Alexander Timpson about the security arrangements. He turned the radio off and lay on the sofa. He was now fed up with listening to the reports of Fenton's tour; he would be glad when it was all over. He closed his eyes and tried to sleep on the sofa.

He felt uneasy. His dreams were now dominated by Vivianne La' Court and with marching up a hill. He could make no sense of it all. He had to get some answers, but he was just going round and round in ever decreasing circles. He did not know what to do.

He could always go out and look for the blonde woman, but he had no idea who she was or where to find her. He could try going to the Red Lion public house again, but who was to say that she would be there. He paced up and down, wondering what to do, then he did what he always did—he put the kettle on.

That night he dreamed he was in a wood. He could hear laughing. Vivianne appeared from behind a tree. He chased after her. He was now beside the canal. Vivianne was in front of him. There was someone else there, up in front of them. He looked at Vivianne—her white dress shimmered in the darkness. She had a sadness in her eyes and a tear rolled down her cheek.

He held out his arms to her. She turned from him and ran towards the distant darkness that soon enveloped them. He chased after Vivianne. She ran to the man who was waiting for her some distance from them. As Gary Taylor approached, he noticed that it was the magician. He held up his hand to stop Gary Taylor then he threw his hand to the floor. There was a big flash of light in front of him. Gary was blinded by the light. He shook his head to clear his senses. Vivianne and the magician were gone.

Gary felt a chill wind. He opened his eyes. He was standing on the canal towpath—he was on the exact spot where Tinky Twinkletoes had been found. He thought he was still dreaming, but no, he was actually there. The last thing he remembered was boiling the kettle. He had no idea how he had got there or what he was actually doing there.

It was cold and it was quiet. He remembered the dream of following Vivianne, and now he stood there himself. He could hear children singing and he flung out his arm. He needed this to stop, but it didn't.

There was a full moon, and it shone brightly, lighting up the towpath. It was like he was now on the stage and the moon was the spotlight—like the sunlight had been for the sock in his bedroom with the light peeping through his curtains, only now he was the ballerina. He flung his arm to the right, bent it at the elbow and then he pulled it across his chest. He was performing, but for whom he didn't know.

This is what he needed to find out—just who, exactly, was pulling his strings.

CHAPTER 12

IN A DARK PLACE

In a darkened room, a puff of smoke went up from a lit cigar. The circle of smoke rose majestically in the gloom. A large man sat behind an oak desk in silent meditation, the curtains drawn to keep the bright sunlight out. His phone rang. "Yes," he answered.

"Someone is trying to access your file."

"Who?"

"She is a filing clerk from the police station."

"Does she have special privileges?"

"No."

"Is she important?"

"Not that we are aware of. She may just be a busy body nosing around,"

"See to it that the file remains closed."

"Yes sir."

The large man took another puff on the cigar and hung up. *Why now?* he thought.

Wayne Taylor wasn't just a doctor; he was a neurologist and a psychologist and had spent years studying neuro brainwaves to see if the right conditions could be met to control the behaviour of people. This would help to understand what makes criminals tick and should be able to amend their ways and put them back on the right path. Wayne Taylor always considered himself to be a good man, doing good things for the benefit of mankind.

Then the Corporation heard about his research, and they knew that they needed this for themselves. And so, they put their fingers on him and persuaded him to change sides.

He had a son, and the only way to protect his son was to work for the Corporation.

Wayne Taylor was now a considerable force within the Corporation, but he could not leave. They still had leverage over him—that was his son. As long as he continued his research for the benefit of the Corporation, his son was safe. But now the Corporation was using his son, and this hurt him. The Corporation had recruited his son without his knowledge. When he had questioned the wisdom of using his son, they said it was to ensure his continued cooperation. And so, he continued his work, but the Corporation had a hidden agenda that even he was not privy to.

———◆━☓━◆———

Two of the men grabbed Gillien by the arms and marched her around the corner, where a third man put a hood over her head and bundled her into a car, which drove off at speed. She heard one of the men tell the driver to slow down——they didn't need to be stopped.

Twenty minutes later, the hood was removed from her head, and she was standing in front of Wayne Taylor.

"So, you're not dead then."

"Neither are you my dear, for the time being at least."

"What are you going to do with me."

"That depends on how cooperative you are."

Wayne Taylor dismissed the men who had brought Gillien in to him and invited her to sit down. She sat as she was instructed to do.

"Why are you investigating me?" he asked.

"We are not investigating you."

"Then why have you opened a sealed envelope?"

"My colleague is investigating your son. We wanted some background information on him. We looked into his parents—they were both listed as dead. We looked to see how they had died, and we got a message to say we couldn't have that information."

Wayne Taylor leaned forwards. "So why didn't you leave it at that and just walk away?"

"Our information was that you were just an ordinary doctor, so why was your death sealed unless the driver of the other vehicle was someone important? That's what we were looking into."

"But I'm not just an ordinary doctor. I specialise in neuroscience."

"What is that exactly?"

"I've been doing experiments on brainwaves to see if we could control the way a person thinks. I was making some progress, when the government got wind of it, and they recruited me to work for them. But it all had to be secret, so they faked my death and sealed the envelope so no one could look into it and find out what I'm doing."

"Your wife, is she still alive?"

"I don't know; I've not had any news about her for several years."

"I could help you find her."

Gillien noticed a subtle change in his demeanour. "Why would you do that?" he asked cautiously.

"Self-preservation," she replied. "You are not going to kill me if I can do something for you."

"You would do this for me?"

"Yes, I would do this for you."

"Why?"

"Because you look like a good guy and seem to have suffered more than most."

Gillien thought she could see a tear in his eye. Now could be the time to find out what they were really up to.

"How does it work, this neuroscience thing?"

"Why do you want to know this?"

"I could help you; then when we've done, I can help you look for your wife."

He sat a while in silent contemplation, not knowing what to do. Gillien knew she had got him, like a fisherman with the big fish on the end of the line she had to wind him in gently so that he wouldn't get away. She knew if this fish got off the hook then it would be the end of the line for her.

"Can you make people do things that they do not want to do?" she asked.

"It's not doing things they don't want to do; it's more like doing things that they don't know they have done."

Gillien thought for a while. "Hypothetically, could someone have killed Adam Hamilton without knowing that he had done it?"

"I suppose that could be possible."

"You mean you're not sure that it could be done, but it would be possible under the right conditions?"

"Yes, but that wouldn't be for the benefit of science and helping to cure mental illnesses."

"So, you are not using this as a weapon then?"

"No. I'm a doctor—I'm here to cure people. I'm trying to find out what makes people tick, so when someone has a serious mental condition, we can treat them and make them better again."

"Who are you working for?"

"I'm working for the government."

"For Matt Fenton?"

"Not him personally but one of the government departments. They're called the Corporation."

"Is this the place on Washington Road?"

Taylor went quiet.

"Are we on Washington Road now?"

Taylor didn't want to say and wouldn't give their location away. He wouldn't say anymore. Gillien knew from his silence that his was exactly where they were. This could be an advantage—knowing exactly where they were. She now needed to get a message out so that Leanne could come and rescue her.

Gillien asked Taylor how his research worked and how he could cure people. Taylor spoke for over an hour about how he had invented a psionic neuro integrator that would allow them to amend a person's brainwaves, and they could use suggestive thoughts to change someone's behaviour patterns. Gillien was taking mental notes of how this all worked—this could be important later, and she would need to get this information to Leanne. A big part of Gillien's work was to remember facts, so when Taylor said something that she didn't understand, she got him to repeat it.

Taylor looked at the woman in front of him. She was a good twenty years younger than he was, around forty-ish, and her hair was cropped short. She was not as thin as she used to be, but she was still attractive enough to captivate Taylor's thoughts. She was intelligent, and she seemed interested in his work and what he was trying to achieve—he liked that about her. She seemed to genuinely be interested in what he was doing. Normally when he talked about his work, if someone didn't understand something, they would just let him ramble on and on until he finished what he was saying. This girl stopped him and asked him to repeat and explain the things that she didn't understand. He wondered if his wife was really gone, could she be the one for him, someone that took interest in his work? But he also had his doubts—could she really like this overweight, smoking man in his advancing years?

She asked him if there were any keywords that could be used to trigger supressed memories or to stop the patient from doing things that he didn't want to do. Taylor was happy to go through all the details with Gillien. They talked for an hour before the guards came and took her away.

"Don't hurt her," he begged. "We will need to talk again."

The guards took her out into the corridor, and one of the guards locked the door behind them. Gillien wondered if Taylor was a prisoner too.

The guards put a blindfold on Gillien and took her up some stairs. She heard a couple of doors open and close as they went down a corridor which echoed as they walked along. Then they stopped. A guard took off her blindfold, opened a door, then he pushed her into a small room. She heard the door lock behind her.

CHAPTER 13

REMEMBER ME

His alarm rang with a shrill chirping sound to signal the start of another new day. Gary Taylor stretched out his right arm and slapped his hand down hard on his alarm clock. There was no clock there, and yet he still heard it ringing.

He went to the bathroom and looked in the mirror. He didn't recognise his reflection. He washed his face and the singing started again. He flung his right arm out and bent it at the elbow. He flung his left arm out and brought his right arm across his chest. He bent the left arm at the elbow, dropped his right arm down by his side, and pulled his left arm against his chest, then dropped his left arm down by his side. The singing stopped.

What is happening to me? he thought. *I must go inside the Corporation.*

He set off and stopped at the junction. "This time," he called out aloud. "This time I'm going in."

Gary Taylor found himself again walking towards the café. The girl, Rose, was sitting at a table outside the café. This time he was going to record their conversation.

Gary approached the girl, Rose, and started recording a video of the conversation on his phone. "Hello," he said.

"Do I know you?" she answered.

"We have met several times."

"If that was the case, you'd think I would remember you, and I cannot place you anywhere in my life."

"We have had this very same conversation every day for the last three weeks, and we will have it again tomorrow. So, for that reason alone, I'm taping this conversation. Then I can play it back to you tomorrow. It may jog something in your memory."

Rose was unsure at first but allowed him to record the conversation. He pointed the phone at the newspaper lying on the table. Then Gary told her about meeting her at the Corporation. Rose had no memory of the Corporation or having ever been there. He told her of their previous meetings, but she had no memory of ever seeing him before. He told her that he would see her again tomorrow, and he gave her a slip of paper. On the paper it said: *My name is Gary Taylor. Remember me. I will see you again tomorrow.*

Gary placed the piece of paper in her handbag and closed it shut.

"I will see you tomorrow. Remember me," he said as he departed.

He had a troubled night that night. In his dreams, children dressed in full military uniforms marched up a hill. He heard the sound of aeroplanes and bombs exploding. He was in turmoil. He saw the children march over the top of the hill, and then they were gone. They did not come back down the hill. He climbed the hill and looked over the other side; all he could see was a sea of blood—bodies scattered everywhere in the distance. Buildings burned; the sky was dark; there was no singing, no screaming; everything was quiet. He looked behind him—everything was normal. He looked in front of him, and everything was in chaos.

He staggered down the blood-soaked hillside. He heard an aeroplane flying above him, then an explosion. He was flung sideways into a bomb crater. There was a girl in uniform, maybe six or seven; she looked more like a majorette than a soldier. She lay face down in a pool of water. He rolled her over; her face was white as a ghost. He picked her up; she lay lifeless in his arms. He could feel pain in his bones, and a tear rolled down his cheek. The tear dropped on to the child, and she opened her eyes wide and started to laugh.

His alarm rang with a shrill chirping sound to signal the start of another new day. Gary Taylor stretched out his right arm and slapped his hand down hard on his alarm clock. There was no clock there, and yet he still heard it ringing. He was shaking from the visions of his dream.

Gary Taylor got up, washed, and ate a quick breakfast. He listened to the radio. Fenton's tour of the country started tomorrow in Coventry. Alexander Timpson was in charge of the security arrangements and didn't expect to see any trouble.

After listening to the full news bulletin, he went down to the café to see Rose. He was going to show her the video of the conversation they had yesterday—maybe this would break the cycle, and he would finally start to get some answers.

He looked puzzled, she was not here; the girl, Rose, was not at the café. He looked around, but there was no sign of her. Then he realised that he never came looking for her; he was always trying to get into the Corporation and had ended up here. He went back down Nelson Lane towards the Corporation. He stopped at the junction. He could see the big green doors closed tight. *This is it*, he thought, *I'm going in.*

He could hear the sound of children singing and brought his right hand up and flung it out to the right. He bent the arm at the elbow and brought his left arm out and flung it to his left before bringing the right arm across his chest. He couldn't stop the movement, so he let it go on. He could hear two voices in the background but couldn't distinguish one from the other. He couldn't make out the words that were being said, but he knew they were talking about him. He knew they were controlling him, and he knew that he had to stop them. He knew he had to see Rose. He felt that she was the key to solving all of this.

Gary Taylor tried to go into the Corporation but again found himself standing down by the canal. He turned around and went back down Wellington Street. *This time*, he thought, *this time more than any other time, I will sort this out.* Again, he found himself standing outside the café, and Rose was there

Gary Taylor introduced himself to the girl, Rose, like he had done every day of this week and the week before that and the week before that. She replied with the same reply, just has he expected. Then he showed her the video of yesterday's conversation and the date on the newspaper on the table, which was yesterday's date.

"This proves we spoke yesterday," he said. "I want you to come back to my place with me."

"Why should I?" she replied. "I don't really know you."

"Then come with me to the Corporation. It is just down this road, only about five minutes to walk it from here. Just take a look we can then come back here for a coffee."

Gary took hold of Rose by the left arm and helped her to her feet. "You have to come with me," he begged of her.

She smiled at him and stood up as he asked. Gary and Rose went down Nelson Lane towards the Corporation. Gary could see the Corporation, the green doors closed tight. "All we need to do," he said. "Is to go inside those green doors; nothing more nothing less."

He could see the doors. He could almost touch them. This was it. He turned to face Rose. "All we have to do is go inside and speak to Domenic, then we can sort this out; then we can go home."

Gary and Rose headed towards the doors of the Corporation ready to confront Domenic Clarkson.

Gary stood in bewilderment; he was not walking back towards the café, nor was he down by the canal, nor was he inside the Corporation. And he didn't have Rose with him either. Instead, he was standing alone outside the police station. Gary had no idea what he was doing there or how he had got there. He could not move for a moment—he was rooted to the spot.

He saw a group of children marching towards him. He ran off in the opposite direction. He didn't want to hear that song; he didn't want to do that movement, not here, not out in the open with everyone looking at him. He kept running until he got home. He went inside and slammed the door shut. He leant against the door, beads of sweat running down his face. He heard a voice in his head say, "He's still trying to resist us."

"Go away," he shouted. "Leave me alone."

The voices continued. "We will have him."

Gary Taylor curled into a ball on the floor, tears in his eyes. "Go away, leave me alone," he pleaded to them, knowing that they could not hear him like he could hear them. He had tried to find answers but had just hit brick wall after brick wall, and now he just wanted it all to end. He didn't have the strength to go on. He could take no more—the dreams disturbed him and he no longer wanted to go to sleep.

CHAPTER 14

GHOSTS

The interview with Taylor had ended abruptly. Meadows had started to act strangely and had turned a whiter shade of pale.

Now, back at the station, WPC Holly Meadows had got her colour back.

"What happened back there?" she asked.

Meadows shook her head. "Something is not right," she said. "Did you feel it?"

"Feel what?"

"Did you feel nothing at all?"

"No, nothing. What happened?"

"I don't know if it was him, the house, or something else, but I definitely felt something."

Meadows looked at Best. "Did you not feel anything?"

Leanne shook her head. "I felt nothing at all."

Meadows got up and started to walk round the room. She looked out of the window. "He's there," she said.

"Who is?"

"Taylor. He's standing outside."

"What's he doing?"

"Nothing, he's just standing there."

Inspector Best came over to the window and there he was—Gary Taylor. He was standing on the other side of the road. Like Meadows had said, he was doing nothing. He was just standing there as if he was in a trance.

"We need to see what he's up to."

Best and Meadows ran outside. When they got out, Taylor had gone. A school teacher marched a class of children past the police station. She smiled sweetly at Best and Meadows and walked on by.

"Where has he gone?" Best said in frustration. Leanne looked up and down the street—there was no sign of Gary Taylor. She turned around, and Meadows seemed to be in a trance. She had her right arm held out to her right. "Are you OK?" she asked.

Meadows was holding her arm out to the right bent at the elbow, pointing in front of her and seemed to stare straight through Leanne. Then she shook her head and dropped her arm.

"What happened to you?"

Meadows just looked at Best and said nothing. The colour had drained from her face again.

"Holly, are you alright?"

"I felt it again as the children walked past."

"I think we need to take you home for a rest."

Leanne Best took Holly Meadows back inside.

Holly looked over her shoulder. Daniel Hobson had his head down, but she felt he was trying to listen in. "I can't say anything here," she said.

"You don't look well, Holly. Do you need me to take you home?" Leanne Best called out in a loud voice so all those around them could hear.

Daniel was tapping on his keyboard as if he hadn't heard a thing, but they both knew he had.

Leanne Best informed Timpson that she was taking Holly home.

"Anything the matter?" he asked.

"No, she is just feeling a little under the weather."

"Will she be alright for Coventry tomorrow?"

"I'm not so sure. It may be best if we take Hobson tomorrow."

Timpson thought about it for a while before agreeing. "He can drive then," he said.

Leanne Best took Holly Meadows home and brewed a nice cup of tea. They sat around the kitchen table. "What's going on?" Leanne asked

"Taylor was up to something in the bathroom, more than just washing his face. I could hear movements which were not consistent to what he should have been doing."

"So, what was he doing?"

"I'm not sure, but I could hear him moving around. When he came out, his demeanour had changed and he didn't want us there, as if he were hiding something."

Holly Meadows was quiet for a moment before she spoke again. "When we started to question him, I could feel something in the house."

"What could you feel?"

"It was a spirit; it turned me cold and shivery, like a ghost had just walked over my grave. It scared me."

Inspector Best looked concerned. She had never seen her colleague like this before. "Can you tell me more?" she asked.

"It's hard to explain. I have an urge to march up a hill, but I do not know where the hill is or why I have to climb the hill. It feels like there is a voice in my head commanding me to march up this hill."

"And Taylor?"

Meadows shook her head. "I have a feeling that this is something to do with him. It all started when we were at his house and happened again when he stood outside the station, just after the children went past."

Best made Meadows comfortable and brewed another cup of tea. They had a chat for about half an hour, then Best got up to leave. She stopped in the doorway. "Call me if you need anything," she said before departing.

Leanne was worried about leaving her friend alone in the state she was in, but she still had work to do, She reluctantly left and went back to the station.

Meadows lay on the sofa with a pillow and a blanket and the radio on low. She tried to rest but couldn't—she had something nagging in the back of her mind but didn't know what it was, and this disturbed her.

The radio was playing a slow romantic ballad, and she could feel herself drifting away.

Meadows fell into a deep sleep, but her dreams were troubled. She was in a full military uniform with a rifle strapped across her shoulder. She was in a line with about ten thousand men. A man was sitting on a horse at the front of the line with a sword in his hand. He marched the soldiers up a big hill. It was an arduous trek; it felt like she was climbing the biggest mountain in the world. When they got to the top of the hill, the duke turned around and marched them down again.

Meadows sensed that she was out of breath and wanted to stop. At the bottom of the hill, the duke turned around and marched them back up the hill. They had only got halfway when Meadows stopped and dropped to her knees. She felt exhausted and couldn't take another step. She could feel herself panting for breath. Another soldier came up to her and helped her to get back to her feet. "You can't stop here," he said. "We have to keep going."

Meadows looked up at the soldier—it was Gary Taylor. "Let me help you. We can do this together," he said.

Holly Meadows woke with a start. She sat bolt upright. The room was dark; the radio was still playing; the digital clock on the radio said it was just past 4 a.m. in the morning. She was cold but was also sweating. Something was not right. *I can't be cold and hot at the same time.*

She got a cup of water and had a sip. Her head was spinning; she couldn't concentrate. The dream felt real, and the emotions were exactly the same as she had felt during the day—a need to climb a big hill—and as she had hinted to Leanne earlier, Gary Taylor was in the thick of it. She couldn't call Leanne at this time of the morning. She would need to call her later. She went back to bed.

Meadows couldn't get back to sleep; the dream had troubled her. There was nothing in his records that suggested Gary Taylor had ever been in the armed forces, but in her dream, he was a soldier, and he told her that they had to go on and that he could help her.

But what did that mean? Was it that she had to continue climbing the hill, or was it something deeper? Was there a mission that he had to complete and was she now a part of it?

———◆◆◆◆———

It was half past nine when Holly got up. The rain was just starting to fall when a car rolled up outside her house. It was Chief Inspector Timpson. He was on the way to Coventry for Fenton's walkabout. She had forgotten about this—Fenton's tour was due to start today.

A door of the car opened and Inspector Best got out. She had come to check up on her. They were on the way to Coventry. Leanne had told Timpson that she wanted to see Holly before they left, and they had to pass her house anyway. Hobson was driving, and Timpson ordered him to stop outside Holly Meadows house. Hobson pulled up and left the engine running.

"I will just be five minutes," Best told them.

Leanne told Holly that they were just on their way to Coventry and expected to be back around 3 p.m. Holly told Leanne about the dream, and that she had seen Gary Taylor in full military uniform. Leanne, like Holly, was not aware of Taylor having ever been in the armed forces. She made a note of it and said that she would check this out when they got back. She advised Holly to take the day off—she was not fit to work today. Leanne told her that she would call in on her when they returned.

CHAPTER 15

SILENCE

Gary Taylor was not sure how long he had been standing in the street outside the police station—it was not where he wanted to be. He had taken Rose from the café to the Corporation. They had never got there, and now he was standing here all alone outside the police station. There was no sign of Rose, and he had no idea where she could be.

Gary surveyed his surroundings. He had been here many times before and nothing looked out of place; everything was as it should be, except that he was where he shouldn't be, and he had no idea how he had got there. Gary saw a group of children with their teacher marching towards him. He ran off in the opposite direction. He didn't want the police to see him doing that silly marching movement that he did every time he heard the children sing that song—they already had their doubts about him; who knows what they would think if he was standing outside the station flinging his arms in all directions.

Gary ran off, he turned down Churchill Avenue. The road was closed to traffic—there were workmen digging a hole in the street. There was no way any traffic could get through; instead all traffic was diverted down Thatcher Way.

Gary Taylor went past a man digging up the street with a jackhammer. Thud, thud, thud it went, banging in his head. The noise stifled him; he could not move. The man stopped what he was doing. "Are you alright there, mate?" he called out.

There was now silence, as the man had stopped drilling. Taylor could hear again. "How do you work with all that noise?"

"Sorry, I can't hear you, mate." The man removed a pair of bright-yellow Ericson ear protectors from his head. "What did you say?" he asked again.

"How do you work with all that noise?"

The man tapped the Ericson ear protectors. "I can't hear a damn thing with these on."

"I need a pair of those for a couple of weeks for a job I'm doing. Where can I get some from?"

"A couple of weeks you say?"

"Yeah, that's right."

"Well you're in luck then. I have a spare pair in my van. My buddy is off work, but he'll be back a week Friday, so I will need them back for then."

The man trotted off to his van. Gary could hear him rummaging around in the back of his van. "Got them," he called out.

He returned carrying another pair of ear protectors and handed them over to Gary Taylor. He tried them on—he could hear nothing at all. Around him, everything was silent. He looked around. He could see people walking by and cars driving down the next street and birds in the sky, but he could hear nothing at all.

Gary looked down the street where he saw the children with their teacher marching towards him, swinging their arms, practicing for Fenton's visit. They were to do a little parade and sing the song for Fenton. They had made a collage of all his achievements, and they were to present it to him during his walkabout.

The children were coming towards him. They were getting closer and closer. He still had the Ericson's covering his ears. He could see that they were marching, throwing their arms to the left and right. For him, it had been a jerking movement—putting his arm out, then putting it out to the right, then bending it at the elbow before pulling the arm across his chest, and then dropping it down by his side. For the children, it was one flowing movement with both arms, and they were all in unison. The teacher was encouraging them to sing, but he couldn't hear them. They marched right past him, and he could see their lips moving, but he didn't hear a word and didn't fling his arms out. Gary smiled a wry smile to himself. *This could work*, he thought.

Gary took the mufflers off and thanked the man. "How long will you be here for?" he asked.

"We will be working on this road for about six weeks, maybe a little less once Burt comes back."

Gary thanked the man again and promised that he would bring the Ericson ear protectors back next week. He then went home. Now it was time to make his plans. He now thought he would be able to get some answers at last.

It took only a few minutes to get home. Gary took the shortcut down by the canal. Gary made a cup of tea and sat listening to the radio with the mufflers by his side.

He heard the sound of children singing and put on the ear protectors. Everything was silent. He couldn't hear the children, and he couldn't hear the radio, and for the first time in days, he didn't flick out his arms and do that silly marching action. Gary Taylor kept the ear protectors by his side all night, then put them on again when he went to bed, and he slept soundly. He had no disturbing dreams; everything was quiet and everything was peaceful. Now he needed to see if he could get into the Corporation and find out what was really going on. He needed to see if he could get there without ending up at the café.

Gary woke with the sound of a warbling alarm clock. He opened a bleary eye; he was still wearing the Ericson ear protectors, but they had come off one of his ears as he slept. Although he had not had the dream that night, he was still disturbed that he heard the alarm clock that was not there. This could mean that whoever was doing this to him was still trying to control him, even though he had shut them out. He knew that if he was going to get the answers he needed, then he needed to keep hold of these until after he had been inside the Corporation. Today was going to be a very important day for Gary Taylor—he could feel it in his bones.

He wondered what he would say to Domenic Clarkson. He needed to find answers, but he couldn't afford to upset Domenic. He would need to be tactful. He sat at his kitchen table with a mug of tea in one hand and a pen in the other. He scribbled down some notes, read them through, crossed them out, and wrote down something else. Gary Taylor had never been confrontational, and finding the right words was difficult for him.

He put the radio on to get some inspiration. The news was about the start of Fenton's tour, which would start today in Coventry. He would have a meeting with the town dignitaries around 11 a.m. before having a short walkabout around town, meeting the people for about thirty minutes and discussing his future plans. Then tomorrow he would be heading north to Sheffield. Alexander Timpson was sure that there would be no repeat of the fracas from similar walkabouts in which several members of the cabinet had been attacked with flour. Timpson had stated that stringent security measures had been put in place, and Fenton would be safe.

Gary Taylor scribbled down his thoughts several times, changing words here and there until he got what he thought he would be able to say to Domenic Clarkson. He put the Ericson's over his ears and put on a black beanie hat to cover them so that he was not too conspicuous. Then he set off for the Corporation. Walking down Wellington Street, he felt sure that now he would get the answers that he needed.

He reached the junction with Nelson Lane and stopped for a while to compose himself, then walked on. Here he was at last standing before the great gates where none shall pass. He pushed and pulled on the gates but they did not move—they remained stubbornly closed. He pulled on the little side gate but that wouldn't open either.

He banged on the gates and called out. "Let me in."

No one answered his calls and the gates remained closed. He decided to wait until someone went in or out of the Corporation, then he would nip in before the gates closed again.

He sat down on the pavement by the side of the gates and waited and waited. He stayed there for over an hour. No one came in and no one came out. He was now getting cold—it had turned a little chilly, and he was not wearing a coat. He stood up, stamped his feet on the ground. He tried the gates again, but they still would not open. He had to find another way in; for now, he was cold and tired. He wanted to stay another ten minutes but decided it would be best to go home. Now he knew he could get to the Corporation. All he needed was a key to get in.

CHAPTER 16

ACCIDENT

Alexander Timpson was getting tied down with the prime minister's grand tour. The attack on Adam Hamilton had now been passed down to Leanne Best and Holly Meadows to look into. Leanne had asked Gillien for a favour, then Gillien went missing. She was not answering her phone and not in her office.

Holly Meadows had been off work for a couple of days. The investigation into the death of Adam Hamilton was going nowhere. Inspector Leanne Best was in a meeting with Alexander Timpson when there was a knock on the door.

"Enter," Timpson called out.

WPC Lisa Barber popped her head round the door. "I hope I'm not interfering," she said, "but we've just had some bad news. Our chief archivist, Julie Gillien, has been killed in a car crash."

The blood ran from Leanne Best's face. She felt quite dizzy. This was her fault; this was something to do with Gillien looking into the sealed envelope for her. Gillien had warned her that they could be stepping on someone's toes if they investigated the sealed envelope.

"Excuse me," she called out and rushed out to the ladies' room, her eyes flooded with tears.

Timpson nodded at Lisa Barber, and she followed Leanne Best to see if she was alright.

Leanne rinsed her face with cold water.

"Are you alright," Lisa asked her.

"I've done this."

"Done what?"

"Gillien was doing something for me."

"What was she doing?"

"I can't tell you because this is what got Gillien killed."

"But she died in a car crash."

"Like hell she did."

Leanne composed herself and went back in to see Timpson. "I need to go out for a short while."

"By all means. She was a friend of yours, take all the time you need."

"Thank you, sir."

Leanne drove down to the mortuary. Mortician Anthony Piggott was on duty. Leanne asked to see him and was taken into his office.

"Good afternoon, what can I do for you today?" he asked.

Leanne Best showed him her ID card. "I'm Inspector Best, my colleague Julie Gillien was killed in an RTA today, and I would like to see the body please."

"Have you got a warrant?" he asked.

"I don't need a warrant to see a dead body."

"You do for this one."

"Why?"

"It's protected."

"By who?"

"I'm sorry, but you do not have the clearance for me to give you that information."

Leanne Best turned away from Piggott; she couldn't bear to hear what he was going to say next. She pulled out her ID and shoved it into his face. "You see this!" she screamed at him. "I have the highest security clearance in the country. Only the Queen is higher than me. Now show me the body of Julie Gillien."

"I'm sorry but I cannot do that."

"Then I will come back with a warrant and the Queen herself if needs be."

Leanne Best stormed out of the mortuary. She stood by her car and counted to ten. She was livid; she kicked the tyre of the car. "Damn you!" she cried out.

She got in the car and drove back to the station. She sat in the car park for about ten minutes. Tears rolled slowly down her cheeks. She knew that Gillien had been killed just like Gary Taylor's parents had been, but why? Then it dawned on her. Gillien must have found something.

She went down to Gillien's office. The door was open. She went in and looked around. She couldn't see anything. "What have you found for me, Gillien?" she asked out aloud.

She stared at the walls for a good ten minutes then looked down at the desk. Gillien had a notepad and it was open. The top page had been torn out of the notepad, but there was an imprint of the message on the next page. Leanne Best took a pencil out of Gillien's drawer and scribbled across the page. The words came to life. In the middle of the notepad just two words said: *not dead*.

"Who's not dead? You're not dead or ..."

The sudden realisation hit her like a slap in the face. The envelope was sealed because Wayne Taylor was not dead, either he was in protective custody, or they gave him a new identity—either way, they have sealed the envelope to stop anyone from finding him. But why could she not see Julie Gillien? Unless ...

Unless Gillien was also not dead, and they had taken her as well. But why take Gillien? Maybe they thought she had found something out, and they wanted to know what we know.

Best thought to herself, *Who can I trust? Do I go to Timpson, or do I have to keep this to myself? Is he in on it? How high does this go? To stop me seeing the body, someone high up has to have authorised this. They would have known I would go to the mortuary and would have instructed Piggott to not let me see the body. Unless there was no body to see. Then he couldn't let me see it. I need to go back to the mortuary.*

Leanne went back upstairs to her desk. *Where is Holly when I need her,* she thought.

She looked around the office; *I need someone to get me a warrant.*

She called over to Daniel Hobson, "Appraisal time, Danny, can I see you in my office."

Daniel Hobson looked surprised. It had been only two weeks since his last appraisal; the next one was not due yet. He knew that Leanne Best didn't like him, but two appraisals in a month—this was taking the biscuit. She had it in for him. He wondered if he should give her a piece of his mind. This was unfair; he was being treated unfairly, and he could take no more. He was thinking of what he would say to her.

"Now, Danny," she barked at him.

Leanne Best went into her office, and Daniel Hobson followed her in. "Close the door please."

Hobson did as he was told and sat opposite Leanne Best. He was steaming inside. He wanted to tell her what he thought, but Leanne spoke first. "Is it hot in here?" she asked.

Before he could answer she said. "Let's go outside for a moment or two." This was not usual for an appraisal. Maybe she was going to sack him. She had seen the way that he despised Holly Meadows, and now she was about to get rid of him. He knew he should have accepted the offer from the Corporation.

Leanne Best went outside. Hobson followed in her wake, expecting the worst. They stood on the steps. Leanne looked up and down the road, then looked up at the office window. "Car park," she said.

They went to the car park. She looked around at the security cameras. She had a feeling that she was being watched.

"There is something I want you to do for me," she said.

"Like what?"

"I want you to get me a warrant to search the mortuary, and you cannot tell anyone about this, not even Timpson. When you have it, bring it to me here."

"Why?" he asked.

"This has something to do with Gillien. I don't think she's dead. You're the only one I can trust—I'm not sure how high this goes. Timpson could be involved. You cannot let him know that you are getting this for me."

The only one I can trust. The words spun around his head. *Maybe I've misjudged Leanne Best all along*, he thought.

Daniel Hobson was gone for about ten minutes. He came back with the warrant.

"Did anyone see you?" she asked.

"No, the office was practically empty. There were only Barber and Morris in."

"What about Timpson?"

"He was on the phone in his office."

"You'd better come with me then—I might need backup."

Leanne drove them to the mortuary. She tried the door; it was locked. She banged on the door; there was no answer. She looked up at the upstairs windows, then knocked on the door again.

"What's up?" Hobson asked.

"The B******d as done a runner," she replied.

"Is this bad?"

Leanne thought about it for a bit. "No, this could be good. This could be the proof that we needed—that Gillien is not dead."

"What do we do now?"

"This is a dead end. I think we need to go back to the station and see if we can find what Gillien found."

She tossed the keys to Hobson. "You can drive," she said.

Hobson drove them back to the station. They went down to the basement and had a look around. Apart from the note that Gillien had left, there was nothing else down there that they could use. If Gillien had opened up the envelope, they either took it with them, or Gillien sealed it up again.

CHAPTER 17

OVER THE TOP

His alarm didn't ring. There was no shrill chirping sound to signal the start of another new day. Gary Taylor didn't stretch out his right arm to slap his hand down hard on his alarm clock. There was no clock there anymore, and today he heard no ringing in his head. He lay contentedly, thinking about the new day. He stretched his arms out wide and slid out of bed He peered through the gap in the curtains and smiled at the world.

Gary Taylor felt excited today—he was going back to the Corporation. Now he would find out what was going on. Taylor had a shower and a light breakfast. He then picked up the ear protectors that the workman had given him.

He set off down Wellington Street until he came to the junction with Washington Road and Nelson Lane. There he could see them—the big green doors of the Corporation.

Gary Taylor had a beanie covering the yellow Ericson ear protectors so that he wouldn't stand out. He walked towards the doors that guarded the Corporation from intruders. Like silent sentries, they stood to attention, not moving a muscle. Taylor walked up to them; he couldn't believe his eyes. Here he was, standing outside the Corporation, not walking briskly to the café for a meeting with Rose.

Taylor pulled on the doors. They were closed tight. Cut into the large door there was a smaller door to allow staff to go in and out without having to open the big heavy gate. Taylor pulled on the door handle, but it was not going to budge. He banged on the Door and called out, "Let me in."

No one answered his calls, and the entry remained barred he could not get in. He now knew that he could get to the gates, all he needed to do was get inside. He decided to wait until someone went in or out.

He sat down on the pavement by the side of the gates and waited and waited. He stayed there for over an hour. No one came in and no one came out. He was now getting cold—it had turned a little chilly, and he was not wearing a coat. He stood up, stamped his feet on the ground. He tried the gates again, but they would not open. He wanted to stay another ten minutes, but it was too cold for him. He had to find another way in.

He looked up at the gates; they were about ten to twelve feet high. He could go over the top, but in the daylight, he would easily be seen. He decided that he had to come back in the dark when no one was around. Now he needed to get warm. Taylor turned around to go back home.

As he walked back up Washington Road towards the junction, he noticed a sensor on the lamp post. It was on this side of the lamp post so wouldn't be visible when he came down Wellington Street. There was also a little black box at the bottom of the lamp post. Across the road, there was the same again on another post, not visible when you approached from the opposite direction. Were these the sensors that were stopping him, or anyone for that matter, entering the Corporation, did they emit a signal to your brain telling you to go down Nelson Lane? Was Rose working for the Corporation? Every time he was sent down Nelson Lane, she was waiting at the café. Yet when he went directly to the café, there was no sign of Rose. Did the sensors send Rose a message to meet him at the café? Was the bit where she didn't recognise him just a decoy to find out what he knew?

The one thing that Gary Taylor did know was that he couldn't trust anyone—not Rose or Domenic. He now needed to go in after everyone had gone home. He needed to make a plan; he would need to go over the gate. He knew that now, with the borrowed ear protectors, he could get to the gate. Now all he needed was to get over the top and find out what they were up to.

Taylor went home. He walked up Wellington Street. There was a blonde woman across the other side. He didn't know who she was, but he had seen her a few times now. He wondered if she was watching him for the Corporation. He went a few yards further and turned around; she was no longer there. He felt that he might be getting a little paranoid—everyone he saw he assumed was working against him.

Gary Taylor arrived home about fifteen minutes later. He checked his shed; he had a step ladder. He took it out of the shed and propped it up beneath his bedroom window. The window ledge was about the height of the gates. He climbed the ladder and reached across for the window ledge. The ladder was not steady and it felt like he was going to topple over. He scrambled down the ladder quickly as he could; the left leg of the ladder had sunk into the soft ground.

He pushed down on the right-hand side of the bottom rung so the ladder was even again, then he climbed the ladder and reached out with his left arm—he could reach the window ledge. He climbed back down the ladder and examined the base. Both legs were sunken about three inches into the soft soil. Outside the Corporation, the ground would be solid, and the ladder would not sink into the ground.

He went to the front of his house and lifted two flagstones from his front drive. They were about fifteen inches square, bulky and heavy. He carried them around to his back garden one at a time. He was bent double as he tried to carry them. He placed the flagstones side by side beneath his window and put the ladder on the flagstones. This would re-create the conditions outside the Corporation. He was not sure but thought he felt the ladder slip a bit when he climbed up.

He was now having doubts. *The ladder could still slip*, he thought. And what about taking the ladder to the Corporation? He would have to carry it there. Gary Taylor picked up the ladder. He wondered how he would be able to take it down to the Corporation. He held it out on front of him and walked around the garden. He couldn't walk down the street like this—it would be too obvious that he was up to something. He held the ladder above his head and tried to walk around the garden. He felt that this was too cumbersome. He held the ladder under his arm, but again, he was having trouble holding on to it. He put his arm through the ladder and rested it on his shoulder; this would be his preferred way to carry it. He walked around the garden. After a few minutes, the ladder was digging into his shoulder and he ached. He put the ladder down on the lawn and decided that if he was to use the ladder, he would need another way to get it down to the Corporation.

He paced about the garden for a moment or two. The ladder was not a good idea—it could get him over the gate but getting it there was too impractical.

He was tired and his muscles ached. He might have over done it, carrying the ladder around the garden. He went inside, put the telly on, brewed a cup of tea, and sat on his sofa. The television was showing an old spy film in black and white. It had already started by the time he sat down, had he been another five minutes, he would have missed a very important part of the story.

In the film the spy had to enter a tall building. He could not go in through the front door. The spy had got a grappling hook, which he threw up on to the roof. When the hook landed, he pulled the rope tight. The hook snagged on the roof ledge. He pulled on the rope to test that it could take his weight then he climbed the wall on to the roof of the building. This was a light-bulb moment. Taylor had seen the way in—he needed a grappling hook. This was not something that he had lying about in his shed and was not something that you could just buy at the local hardware store. He needed to figure out where he could get one from.

He sat and watched the film to the end. He had no idea what the film was about. The one thing that stood out for him was the use of the grappling hook. It was too late to do anything about it now; he would wait until the morning. For the second night in a row, he slept soundly. The ear protectors were working.

CHAPTER 18

THE GRAND TOUR

His alarm rang with a shrill chirping sound to signal the start of another new day. Matt Fenton stretched out his right arm and slapped his hand down hard on his alarm clock. Today was to be the start of his grand tour around the country. He was to visit twelve cities in sixteen days, starting today with Coventry. His idea was that he would travel down on the day of the tour to each town. Appleyard had told him that this was not a good idea in light of what had happened to him and had advised that he should go down to Coventry the day before, stay in a hotel, and go over his schedule that night. "You need to be prepared," Appleyard told him.

Fenton reminded Appleyard that Timpson would be travelling down on the day, and he was confident of Timpson's abilities to make sure that everything ran smoothly. After all, he had the assurances of Timpson's brother, Jonathan, the minister for home security, that nothing would go wrong on the tour, and that was good enough for him.

"I trust both men," he told Appleyard.

The first day of the tour, Daniel Hobson would drive Timpson and Best to Coventry, but first Leanne wanted to call in on Holly to make sure that she was alright—it was on their way and would only take five minutes. Timpson agreed that Leanne should call in on Holly. Hobson was not pleased that they would have to make an unscheduled stop on the way. He had never really got on with Holly Meadows. He always viewed her as a rival, and she was getting all the breaks. This was his time to shine, and still, she was taking the shine off it.

Hobson drove up to Holly Meadows's house and sat impatiently in the car with Timpson. He left the engine running to let Leanne Best know that he was waiting. She went inside, seemed to be in for ages and ages, but it was really only about ten minutes until Leanne came back to the car. Leanne told them that Holly was feeling much better, but she had given her the day off anyway. The last thing Hobson wanted was them talking about Meadows all the way to Coventry, so he tried asking about what the arrangements would be once they got to Coventry.

Timpson told Hobson to concentrate on the road and continued to quiz Best about Meadows's condition. They reached Coventry and were greeted by Coventry's chief Constable, Mahmood Singh, who escorted them to the council chambers where Fenton was already in discussions with the mayor. Introductions were made, and Timpson went over the planned route with Fenton and the mayor.

Best and Hobson went out on to the streets to check the route through the town centre. There was only a small crowd, about fifty to a hundred people at the most, and six of Coventry's finest officers lined the route that Fenton would be travelling.

Hobson looked at the small gathering. "Even if he speaks to everyone in the crowd, this walkabout shouldn't take long."

Best had to agree. If Taylor turned up here, they would easily be able to spot him in such a small crowd.

The walkabout in Coventry went ahead with no issues. Hobson drove them back and dropped off Leanne at Holly's house. She needed to know that Holly was OK.

They got to Holly's house at around three thirty, just half an hour after Leanne's estimated time that they would be back. Holly was up and doing some cleaning. She'd had a good day; nothing had gone off today, and she had not had any more visions. Everything had been back to normal. Even so, Leanne advised her to take a couple more days off, just to be on the safe side.

The following day, the tour moved on to Sheffield. Lisa was the driver today—Leanne had decided that they would rotate the driving schedule. There was a bigger and more enthusiastic crowd waiting for Fenton today. The people of Sheffield welcomed Fenton, and there were several hundred in the crowd.

Timpson stayed near to Fenton. The Sheffield police were stationed along the route. Leanne Best patrolled down one side and Lisa Barber down the other side. There was no sign of Gary Taylor, and little trouble. The people were eager to see Fenton and were pushing to get to the front. Luke Appleyard had come up to Sheffield, and he walked with Timpson a few yards behind Fenton.

Timpson scanned the crowd as they walked along; there was no sign of Taylor. Timpson knew that Taylor would turn up sooner or later. This was now two cities down with ten to go.

The walkabout had taken longer than the one at Coventry, but Fenton was building up momentum. Appleyard had thought it was folly to tour the country but now was not so sure—the crowds seemed to be on their side.

There was a day off on day three; then day four saw them heading to Manchester. The visit to Sheffield had garnered favourable media coverage, and the crowds at Manchester were even bigger. Timpson took it in his stride. Best and Morris were surprised at the size of the crowds, which were now getting into the thousands. Again, Timpson walked behind Fenton but this time not with Appleyard. It was the transport minister, Debra Travis, who had accompanied Fenton to Manchester. They scanned the crowds; Morris and Best saw no sign of Taylor.

On the way home, Best suggested that if it was Taylor that was going to attack Fenton, maybe they were wasting their time at these walkabouts, as Taylor didn't drive. If he was going to strike, it would be at the venue on their home patch. Timpson had to agree with Best that this was the most likely scenario. Even so, they still had to offer protection for Fenton, and they would continue to do so.

The following day, Hobson drove them up to Newcastle, and again the crowds were getting and bigger and bigger. If the election was tomorrow, then Fenton would surely walk it. The tide had turned—it was now in his favour.

Ten dates down in thirteen days; there were only two left. It was a day off today, Brighton tomorrow, and then their home patch at Milton the day after tomorrow, which is where they would expect Taylor to strike.

Up to now, there had been no sign of any trouble and, more importantly, no sign of Taylor. This is how Timpson wanted it; he needed another quite day tomorrow, and then they could concentrate on the last day.

Holly Meadows was back at work, but Leanne had assigned her to desk duties whilst the tour went ahead. She didn't want anything to happen to Holly, especially whilst she was not there to look after her.

Leanne called in on her every day. Holly was getting back to her usual self now that she was back at work. Leanne had asked Hobson to keep an eye on Meadows to make sure she was OK.

Hobson didn't want to do babysitting duties. He sat at his desk, filling in his daily routine report. Nothing much had happened today. He glanced up and Holly Meadows was looking across at him. "We need a holiday," she said.

"Who does?" he replied.

"All of us. This has been a stressful few weeks, and we could all do with a little holiday to cheer us up and get us back into the mood again."

"I'm OK as I am."

"OK, if you say so."

"What does that mean?"

"I've seen you skulking away behind your desk. I'm no fool. I can see you're unhappy."

"I'm worried about Gillien," he lied.

"Do you think we will ever see her again?" Holly asked.

"Alive?" he countered.

It suddenly dawned on Holly that they had not seen or heard from Gillien in over three weeks, and she could be dead. She wondered if Taylor had done it—killed Hamilton, killed Gillien, and now after Fenton.

<hr />

No one from the force had seen Taylor for several days. This made Timpson nervous. "If Taylor is not out and about then he is hiding away planning something."

Best agreed and thought that Taylor was getting ready to strike. Both agreed that the strike would come the day after tomorrow. Lisa Barber was doing the driving for the last time tomorrow. Hobson had finished his stint. It would be Morris again for the last day, although there wouldn't be much driving, as the square was within walking distance of the station. Timpson's brother, Jonathan, would also be at the last walkabout as would Appleyard, who would also be there at Brighton tomorrow.

Being on high alert for such a long time was taking its toll on Leanne Best. She was exhausted and was glad there were only two more days to go. There was still no news on Gillien and still not enough evidence to get Taylor for the attack on Hamilton.

After three weeks, the trail was getting cold. If Taylor did show up in the next two days then things could quite easily heat up again.

CHAPTER 19

PLAN B

His alarm rang with a shrill chirping sound to signal the start of another new day. Gary Taylor stretched out his right arm and slapped his hand down hard on his alarm clock. There was no clock there, and yet he still heard it ringing. The ear protectors had come off and were beside on him in the bed.

He sat up. The ear protectors had worked. He knew now that he could get to the Corporation Taylor now needed something to get him over the gates at the Corporation so that he could have a look around and see what they were doing. Taylor had decided that he would go over the gate once it was dark, and he needed something to get him over the gate. A ladder would be too cumbersome and would be difficult to carry and would probably cause suspicion if he was seen. He needed something more simple that would be easy to carry and harder to detect. He was going to need something like a grappling hook, but to get one of these would also raise suspicion. He didn't need a long piece of rope; he only needed something that he could grab on to so that he could get over the top of the gate. He decided that maybe he would be able to make one himself. He was sure that he had a length of rope in his shed.

Gary Taylor spent an hour or two rummaging around in his shed. He did find a length of rope about eight or nine feet long. He found a sort of three-pronged hook which had at one time been a gardening implement. He now needed to attach this to the rope and he would be set to go. The rope was too thick to tie it on the hook, so he had to improvise.

Gary Taylor found an old washing line. He was not an expert when it came to knots, but he tied the line as best as he could to the hook. Then there was the tricky part—he had to tie the line to one end of the rope. He undid the bit on the hook. He decided to fix the rope by first putting the end into a loop and tying it into place with the washing line. It didn't need to be a good job; it just needed to be good enough to take his weight for about ten minutes as he scrambled over the gates at the Corporation.

He cut the line when he had finished the loop, then tied the remainder to the hook and threaded it through the loop and back on to the hook again. It had taken about an hour to do, but he was satisfied that it was secure enough to get him over the gate. He needed to try it out to see if it would take his weight, just like the spy had done in the film that he had watched the night before.

Gary Taylor fixed the hook to his bedstead, then lowered the rope out of his window and went outside. The rope ended just above his head. He reached up, grabbed the end of the rope, and pulled up his legs. If the rope was not strong enough to take his weight then this was the time to find out. It held firm. Taylor went inside and unhooked the grappling hook from his bed. The bars on the bedstead had bent slightly, but the hook had held firm to the rope. Taylor was pleased with his handiwork.

Now all he had to do was to wait for it to get dark. He was reading a book when he heard the sound of children singing. He quickly put on his ear protectors and the singing was gone. All around him was silence—he could hear nothing at all.

Taylor had a nap on the sofa. He had a troubled dream: two men in white coats were standing over him. He knew that they were doctors, but he couldn't hear a word they were saying. When he woke up, it was already dark. The ear protectors had come off one of his ears. He lay in a contorted position and ached; it felt has if he had been rolled up in a small box. Taylor looked at his clock—it was well past midnight.

He looked out of the window and wondered if he should go out, as it was very late. Then he realised that was the plan all along was to go out when it was dark and no one was around. This was the perfect time to go out.

Taylor wrapped the rope over his left shoulder; he needed his right arm to be free to move. He then put on a dark overcoat, making sure that he covered the rope so it could not be seen. The hook was digging into his side. He twisted the hook so that the prongs were facing away from his body. He put on a dark beanie hat to cover the yellow ear protectors. He wore dark walking boots. He would need the grip of some strong boots to scale over the gate.

Taylor closed the curtains and turned off all the lights. He wanted it to look like he had gone to bed.

Then he slipped silently out of the back door. Like a cat stalking its prey, he crept around the side of the house. He couldn't hear anything. He tripped on the drive where he had removed the flagstones and cursed under his breath. If this was to work, he couldn't afford to be clumsy and keep tripping up like this. He kept his eyes peeled. At the corner of the house, he held back in the shadows and looked up and down the street. He could see no movement. He rushed down to his gate in a half-crouched position.

He stopped at his gate and looked up and down the street again. He looked at the windows of the houses across the road—all was still. He set off down the street at a brisk pace. The hook had turned again and one of the prongs was sticking into his side. He pulled up behind a bus shelter and adjusted it again, then carried on. He looked at his watch—it was now just before 1 a.m. He saw a fox pad across the street. He had never seen a fox before and watched as it silently went on his way. Had he not been out at this time, he would never have seen an urban fox. Like the fox, he walked silently through the streets towards his final destination, the mighty Corporation. They would not see him coming this time.

He reached the gates of the Corporation, undid his coat, and removed the home-made grappling hook. He had made it so far; it was now time to see if his plan would work.

He fastened his coat and threw the hook into the air, but it missed its target and fell harmlessly to the ground. The next two attempts failed as well.

He let out more rope and tried again. On the fourth throw, the hook went over the top of the gate. Had he not been wearing the ear protectors, he would have heard a dull clanking sound, which was not right. He pulled on the rope and the hook snagged on the top of the gate. The rope came down to just below his chest. He tugged on the rope again; he was satisfied that the rope was secure and pulled himself up hand over fist. With his feet firmly gripping the wooden door, he hurled himself upwards. He grabbed the top of the gate and pulled himself up.

He straddled the top of the gate like a cowboy sitting on his horse. The gate had a wooden appearance at the front, but the back of the gate was reinforced steel.

Gary Taylor unhooked the grappling hook and threw it to the ground. He then lowered himself down the back of the gate and allowed himself to drop the last couple of feet into the courtyard.

He coiled up the rope and hid it in a dark corner by the gate. The moonlight cast a silver glow on the yard. Gary stayed in the shadows and glanced around; it was well after 1 a.m., and there was no sign of movement anywhere. He dashed across the yard to the main entrance. Gary turned the handle of the door and pulled hard. The door was locked and would not open. He pulled on it again and still it would not open. He peered through the window; all he could see was a long corridor backing into the distance. He pulled and pushed on the door; it would not budge. He examined the window, but it was closed tight. He cursed under his breath for the second time that night. Things were not going to plan—he had got into the Corporation's inner courtyard, but he had now come to a dead end. He looked around in frustration. He needed a plan B.

CHAPTER 20

AN OPENING

Gary Taylor sat on the steps outside the Corporation. The door was locked, the window too. He had come to a dead end. He sat there for quite a while thinking there had to be another way in. It was now 2 a.m.—he had been here for almost an hour.

He walked back out into the courtyard and looked the building up and down. About twenty yards to the left was a building that looked like it had been added on, and there was a window half open. He would need to climb a little ledge to get to it; he thought this was doable. He climbed on to the ledge, prized the window open further, and peeped inside. It looked like it was a ladies' powder room. He would not get in wearing his heavy overcoat, so he climbed down from the ledge. He put his beanie hat in the coat pocket, then took off his coat and folded it up and placed it in the dark corner with the grappling hook. He climbed the ledge and put his head and shoulders through the window. He reached out with his arms, grabbed the side of a cubicle, and pulled himself through the window.

He didn't want to be seen in a ladies' powder room that would not do at all. He rushed to the door, opened it a little, and looked out into the corridor. He could see nothing at all. He opened the door a little more and poked his head out. He looked up and down the corridor—there was no movement; all was still. The coast was clear.

He walked quickly down the corridor to the main entrance and undid the latch; this would now be his way out. He went down the corridor and saw some stairs climbing upwards. He remembered that this was the way to the auditorium. Gary Taylor climbed the stairs until he reached a landing.

The stairs continued to go up, but here on the landing was the door to the auditorium. He opened the door and slipped inside. It was dark; he couldn't see anything.

He fumbled around the doorway and found the light switch. He turned on the lights and the auditorium lit up. He walked over to the seat where he had sat on that fateful day when he was last there.

Everything that had happened to him since had started after that day. He sat down in his seat. In his mind's eye, he could see Domenic Clarkson running up the stairs and pointing in his direction. Why was he pointing? Was he saying something to him? Was he coming to him or was he giving instructions? He could now see Rose coming down the aisle to sit next to him. Was this it? Was he planting her next to him? Was she part of the master plan?

He thought about the meetings at the café. She was only there when he had been turned away from the Corporation. She wasn't there when he went straight to the café? Were the sensors a message for her to go to the café?

She just had to be a part of it—he was now convinced of it. When the doctors called out for volunteers, they were always going to take Rose. Had Clarkson sat next to him to say to the doctor "Take this one as well"?

Gary Taylor ambled down to the stage like he had done when the doctor had taken him. He remembered that he went through a side door into a small room, possibly a dressing room, at the side of the stage.

The door to the little side room was still there at the side of the stage, Taylor went inside. The light switch was at the side of the door. He turned on the light; the room was how he remembered it, with the large table in the middle of the room. He went over to the table as he had done before. The doctor had told him to follow Rose through another door. He remembered being sprayed with water as he went through the door. Gary Taylor went were to the door should be but it was not there—the wall was solid brick, and there was no other door in the room. The only door was the one that he had come in from. He remembered the door in the wall going outside and climbing the hill before being called back. He spun around. "This is not right," he called out to no one in particular.

He banged on the wall; it was solid brick. There was no sign of a door in this wall, but he knew it was there—he had been through the door.

There were three slot windows on the top of the wall about six inches deep and two feet across. They were too high to see out of. There was a pole in the corner of the room to open the windows. Gary Taylor pushed the desk up to the far wall and climbed on to the table. He looked out the window, but there was no courtyard. There was a big drop of about twenty to thirty feet to a grassy lawn. "This cannot be. I went out there," he said to himself.

Taylor sat on the table and thought about the spray and the sensors that stopped him coming back to the Corporation. Was the same thing done here? Had he been tricked again?

He remembered going back out into the auditorium and the presentation had finished. It had been on for two hours, but to him it felt like he had only been in the room for five minutes something had happened here, and he did not know what.

Taylor remembered the doctor taking something out of the back of his hand. He had scraped his hand with a pair of tweezers and had removed a capsule that had been ten millimetres long and about two millimetres in diameter. He had removed another from the other hand. This was where his hands now itched, and he started to scratch the backs of his hands again.

He had followed Rose back into the auditorium. Gary went back out and exited the auditorium. If he left now, he would not have found what he was looking for. Instead of going down, he went up the stairs. At the top there was a double door with a glass window. He looked through the window—there was a brightly lit corridor. Gary Taylor pushed on the doors, and they opened. He was not expecting that; he assumed that they would be locked.

Gary Taylor went through into the corridor. There were five doors on the left-hand side of the corridor. The first two rooms were empty. He looked through the window of the door into the third room. It was dimly lit. In the third room, he could see six hospital beds with people hooked up to monitors. Gary Taylor couldn't see who was in the beds. He cautiously entered the room and went to the first bed. He didn't know the man in the bed but recognised his face as one of the six that were taken to the room on that first day at the Corporation. He lay motionless as if he were in a coma.

He went to the second bed. Rose was in the second bed. She lay there as the first man had done. He gave her a gentle shake, but she did not

93

move. He removed the ear protectors and let them hang around his neck. He spoke softly to Rose. "Rose, can you hear me?"

Rose did not stir, he gave her another gentle shake, but again, she did not move.

It was now 3 a.m. Without the ear protectors on, he could hear every movement in this silence. He could hear Rose gently breathing, but he couldn't wake her. He removed the two fine electrodes from her forehead and followed the wires to a small unit at the end of the bed. Another wire led to a computer on a desk in a dark corner at the back of the room. He walked past the other four beds without taking any notice of who was in the beds. As he approached the desk, he heard the sound of distant footsteps heading his way.

Gary Taylor crouched down behind the desk just as the door opened. Two men in white coats walked into the room. He didn't know them, but he recognised the voices. These were the voices he had heard in his head behind the children singing. He couldn't hear exactly what they were saying. He strained to listen in. He thought one said, "We only have two days to get it right."

To which the other replied, "It's all right. We have him now. He is ours."

One of them noticed that the electrodes had come off Rose's head and reattached them.

Gary Taylor sat on the floor with his head bowed down resting in his hands. He was willing the men to go away; he didn't want to get caught here.

CHAPTER 21

GONE TO GROUND

Her alarm rang with a shrill chirping sound to signal the start of another new day. Holly Meadows stretched out her right arm and slapped her hand down hard on her alarm clock; the ringing stopped. Holly Meadows had been off work for a week since she had visited Gary Taylor at his home. Now it was time to go back to work.

Matt Fenton had started his daily walkabouts. He would be here in a few days. She needed to be ready. Leanne had checked in on her every day that she had been off, and now that she was back, Leanne had placed her on desk duties until after Fenton's tour had finished. She had asked Hobson and Barber to keep an eye on her whilst she was out with Timpson. She knew that something was going to happen on the final day and didn't want Holly to get hurt in the crossfire. They knew that Gary Taylor was involved and that they had to stop him. Holly had not had the dream or the feelings for several days now, so it was decided that she could come back to work and help out from the station. She could check the leads they had on Hamilton and Taylor. Holly didn't mind, she was just glad to be back, even if she was not in the thick of the action. To be doing anything at all was better than moping around at home.

Leanne and Timpson had just come back from Bristol. This was the last of four dates for Hobson; tomorrow was a rest day. The day after that, Barber would be taking them down to Brighton. Then it was back here to Milton for the last date of the tour. No one had seen or heard anything from Taylor for a few days now. Timpson was worried—they could see it in his face. He marked off another tour day on the calendar.

Leanne asked if there was any news of Gillien. No one had seen or heard from her in three weeks. Leanne knew that she had been taken, but no ransom requests had been made. Maybe Gillien knew too much, and they would not hear anything until after Fenton had been taken out. Maybe they were holding her because she knew their plans.

The thought encouraged Leanne Best to stay positive, but in the back of her mind, she feared that Gillien could already be dead.

Holly had not had a dream about Taylor for several days. Now, with it getting close to the day when Fenton would be here, she had the dream—climbing the hill with Taylor by her side, him in a military uniform carrying a gun. She needed to tell Leanne about it.

Holly Meadows arrived at work bright and early. There was no sign of Leanne Best. She asked Daniel Hobson if he had seen Leanne. "She went out early," he said.

"Do you know where to?"

"She didn't say."

Holly Meadows sat at her desk for a while, Alexander Timpson called her in to do a return-to-work form. He completed the form, asking all the usual questions. Then they discussed the security arrangements for Matt Fenton's visit. He asked if she was alright with being taken off the protection rota. She agreed that it was for the best, and she was OK with letting the others go in her place.

She went back to her desk. There was still no sign of Leanne Best.

<hr>

Holly Meadows was sitting at her desk. She had the file on Gary Taylor in front of her, but she wasn't reading it.

Daniel Hobson approached her. "Are you alright, Hol? You look distracted."

She looked up from her desk. "Yeah, fine," she replied. " I'm just having problems sleeping. A little tired, that's all."

"Me too."

"I keep having this same dream over and over again."

"About marching up a hill?"

Holly looked at Daniel with a quizzical look. "Yeah that's right, how could you know that."

"I've been having the same dream." Daniel pointed at the folder in front on Holly. "Only last night this guy was in my dream too." Daniel sat on a chair opposite Holly. "I woke up just after three in the morning and couldn't get back to sleep."

Daniel could see the colour visibly draining from Holly's face. "Are you alright, Hol?"

"I need a drink of water."

Daniel fetched her a cup of water and placed it on the desk beside her. She took a big swing then looked at Daniel. "When did you first have this dream?"

"It was a few weeks ago now."

Holly was not expecting this; she had only been having the dream for a few days, since she had visited Gary Taylor at his house with Leanne Best. "Do you know exactly when the dreams started?"

"I don't know the exact date, but I do remember when they started."

"Tell me when."

"It was just after we moved into this building. I was not enjoying my job, so I went for an interview at a place called the Corporation."

Daniel paused for a moment to compose himself. "The strange thing is I can't remember anything about the interview. I've tried to go back to the place but cannot remember where it is."

Holly scribbled down a few notes to remind her later on. She needed to discuss this with Leanne when she came back. Daniel remembered something else.

"It was around that time when that funny man died. You know; the one with the shiny suit."

"Adam Hamilton?"

"Yeah, but he called him by another name."

"Who did?"

Daniel pointed at the folder again. "This guy here."

"You've met Gary Taylor?"

"Yeah, he was at the station. I took him into the interview room when Leanne interviewed him. He said the strange man was his friend, but Leanne wasn't impressed. He didn't even know the guy's real name."

"We need to see Leanne. I think Taylor has taken Gillien."

"Do you want me to go to this guy's house?"

"No, I think that could be too dangerous."

Then Leanne Best walked into the room. Holly and Daniel told her about the conversation they'd just had—about sharing the same dream, and Taylor, at the heart of it, carrying a gun. Leanne decided that they should go to Taylor's house. Daniel Hobson drove them there.

Leanne stumbled on the drive where two flagstones were missing. Daniel caught her so that she didn't fall flat on her face. Leanne knocked on the door. There was no answer. She knocked louder and called through the letter box, but still there was no answer. Holly looked through the front window—there was no one in the front room. Daniel went round the back of the house. The two missing flag stones were in the back garden under the window. A ladder lay strewn across the lawn. Leanne and Holly came around the back just as Daniel was picking up the ladder and placing it on the flagstones. "I'll hold the ladder if you want to go up," he called out.

Daniel held the ladder and Holly climbed up. For the first time, Daniel and Holly were working as a team. For Daniel this felt good; it was the first time that he had felt involved and valued.

Holly climbed to the top of the ladder. The curtains of Taylor's bedroom were drawn, but she could see through a gap in the curtains. She could see a discarded sock on the floor, the bed unmade. She could detect no movement, and there was no sign of Taylor. She could tell that he was not in and probably had not been in for a couple of days. Holly came back down. Leanne looked in through the kitchen window—he was not there either.

Gary Taylor was not in, a ladder was in the garden, and flagstones were moved from the front of the house to the back. Something did not add up.

Could Taylor have been abducted like Gillien? Or was it as Timpson surmised: that he had gone to ground and was hiding until the day of the attack. They needed now to be on full alert.

Leanne called into the station and informed Timpson that Taylor had gone to ground. The attack was imminent; the expected attack would take place the day after tomorrow, when Fenton was in town.

CHAPTER 22

JUST ANOTHER DAY

His alarm rang with a shrill chirping sound to signal the start of another new day. Gary Taylor stretched out his right arm and slapped his hand down hard on his alarm clock. There was no clock there, and yet he still heard it ringing. The ear protectors had come off in the night again—they were not made for sleeping in.

On the bedside cabinet, where the clock used to stand, there was now a pistol. Gary Taylor sat up with a start. "Where the hell did that come from?" he called out in anguish.

Gary Taylor examined the gun. He emptied the chamber—there were five bullets and six chambers. The gun had been fired, but by who and what at? He had never seen the gun before today. Was someone trying to set him up for something?

The police had said he was the number one suspect in the attack on Tinky Twinkletoes, but they had no evidence. Were they now planting it on him?

Or had the person who had actually attacked Tinky set it up for the police to find him with the gun?

All he knew was that he had to get rid of the gun. There was a knock at the door. He looked out of the window—it was that police woman, Inspector Best.

She had come round early to see if she could catch him in, and he was home. She was not convinced that he was hiding from them and thought she may have better luck if she went round on her own. She could see that he was home; he had nowhere to go. He couldn't run, so his only option was to open the door.

He still had the gun in his hand. He didn't know what to do. He put the gun under the pillow on his bed, removed the ear protectors from around his neck, and went to the door.

"I can't tell you any more about Tinky."

"That's not why I'm here."

"Oh, come in then. What can I do for you today inspector?"

"Is your father still alive?"

"I hope not, I went to his funeral."

"This is serious. I have reason to believe that your father didn't die in a motor accident."

Gary Taylor sat in his chair. "What about my mother?"

"We have no information on your mother yet."

"And why do you think my father is still alive?"

"I've received information from a colleague that he may not be dead."

"Can I ask why you believe this colleague then?"

"She has disappeared the same way that your father did. I've been told that she has died in an automobile accident, but I've been denied permission to see the body."

"Why has this got anything to do with me?"

"We cannot find Vivianne La' Court either. We're trying to join the dots. Your father, your ex-girlfriend, your friend that was killed, and a police officer investigating all of them—the lines point straight at you. You are connected to everyone that is involved in my investigation."

"My father died seven years ago. I do not know the police woman. Tinky was my friend and was still alive when I last saw him. And I've not seen Vivianne for a few years now, although I have been dreaming about her a lot lately."

This made Leanne take notice. She leaned forwards. "Tell me about the dreams."

Gary started to fidget. He was wringing his hands. "Can we do this later?" he asked.

"No, you have to tell me now about these dreams."

"I have to go to the bathroom."

Gary Taylor got up and rushed to the bathroom. He had barely closed the door when he flung out his right arm before pulling it across his chest. Then he flung out his left arm, and he dropped his right arm. He pulled up his right leg, bent at the knee. As he pulled his left arm across his chest, he dropped his right leg to the floor. As he dropped his left arm, he raised his left leg, and as he dropped his left leg, he started again with his right arm. The singing in his head was intense and louder than he had ever heard it before. He felt as if his head was about to explode. In the background he heard a voice say, "We have him."

The second voice said, "Is he good to go?"

The first voice replied, "Yes."

But the singing didn't stop, and he repeated the actions for a third time. Then it all went quiet. He looked in the mirror and saw himself, in a military uniform, looking back. He rinsed his face twice. He could hear the police woman calling him; he went back out.

"My word, you look shocking," said Leanne Best.

"It's just a bug that I've picked up. I need a little fresh air, and then I should be alright."

Leanne figured that she would get no more from Gary Taylor. She thanked him for seeing her and decided to make her way back to the police station. She was sitting outside in her car when Taylor's front door opened. Gary Taylor came out wearing bright-yellow ear protectors. "What the hell," Leanne Best exclaimed to herself.

She watched Taylor walk down the road. Then she got out of her car and followed at a discreet distance. He was walking faster than her and pulling away—that didn't matter as long as she could see where he was going.

Gary Taylor stopped near to where some roadworks were taking place. He felt a tap on his shoulder and spun round. There was a man talking at him, but he couldn't hear what he was saying.

Gary Taylor removed the ear protectors. "Good as your word," the man said. "Burt is back today and he will be needing these."

Gary Taylor had not intended to bring back the ear protectors. He was just walking aimlessly and had ended up here. Taylor handed back the ear protectors to the workman. "Thank you, they were most useful."

"In truth you could have had them another day. We are not working tomorrow on account of that politician doing his walkabout."

Taylor had no idea what he was doing here; he had not intended to come out. He remembered waking up with the gun by his bed, that he needed to get rid of it, but he had not brought it out with him. Maybe he was just looking for somewhere to dispose of it.

Gary Taylor looked around. He could see a teacher marching children down the street with made up uniforms. They were singing that damn song. He needed to get out of here. He turned around and could see the police woman walking down the street. He feared that she was following him. He ran off down a side street.

Leanne Best was following Gary Taylor. He was quite a way in front of her. Then he stopped to talk to a workman. She slowed down but continued to walk towards him.

After a short conversation with the workman, he handed over the bright-yellow ear protectors. Then he turned round and he saw her. He took off like a bat out of hell, heading down Winston Lane. Leanne Best gave chase, but he had a head start. She saw him turn left at the end of the lane. She ran down the lane and turned left. She saw him turn right down another street; she turned right. It was only a short lane; she ran down to the end of the lane. She was on Wellington Street. The street was deserted. There was no sign of Gary Taylor—he had got away. She walked back to where the workmen were; they were packing up for the day.

"A short day today," she said to the workman Taylor had spoken to.

"What's it to do with you?" he replied.

She showed him her ID.

"It's all down to that politician coming tomorrow. We have to pack up today, clear around here, and start again on Monday."

Leanne Best pointed at the yellow ear protectors "Who was the guy that gave you these?" she asked.

"Dunno his name," the workman replied. "He borrowed them sometime last week."

"What did he want them for?"

"He said he was doing a job, and it was too noisy for him to concentrate. He asked if he could borrow them and said he would bring them back today, which he has done."

Leanne thanked the man for his time and went back to find her car, which she'd left outside Taylor's home. If Taylor was going to attack

Fenton in the square, why did he need a ladder? And why would he need ear protectors? Unless he was going to be up high in a noisy place—like a clock tower that might chime at the time of the attack. Leanne rushed back to her car; she needed to check the clock tower in the square.

CHAPTER 23

ESCAPE

Julie Gillien had no idea how long she had been held or even where she was. From the conversations with Taylor, she assumed that she was on Washington Road. It was only about ten minutes from the police station but it had taken twenty minutes to get there by car. Maybe they drove around the block a couple of times to confuse her. She had been here long enough—she had got plenty of information from Taylor and had made many mental notes about his work. She didn't want to outstay her welcome; she decided now was the time to get out.

Julie Gillien looked around the room one last time. The room was about a ten foot square and had just one window. There were bars on the window and shutters that were closed from the outside, so she could not see out. There were sparse furnishings in the room—a bed, a bedside cabinet, and a small table. She was allowed out twice a day to go to the washroom, where two guards would stand over her whilst she washed herself. She had not had a change of clothing, and in truth, she felt she was starting to smell a bit.

She had spoken with Taylor a few times and had gained his confidence. He had told her quite a bit about his psionic neuro integrator systems. She just hoped that she could remember it all once she had got out. She felt that she had got a good grip of the principles of the system and what they were trying to do with it, but felt that the Corporation and Taylor had differing views on how to use it.

Gillien had managed to get a nail out of the wall and also had a hairgrip. She figured that she would be able to pick the lock, but the hair grip didn't have enough strength to do this and just bent as she tried it. She was making better progress with the nail. Eventually, she heard the lock click. Gillien slowly opened the door and took a peak outside. There was no one guarding the door. She took a cautious step outside. She wondered where the guards were—there was no sign of them. She closed the door behind her.

Gillien felt a shiver of trepidation—she was a filing clerk not a hero. This could see her escape to freedom or get shot in the process, and she didn't want that. She could sit tight and see it through, but there were no guarantees that they would let her go. She had Taylor's word that no harm would come to her, but she was not sure how much weight he carried or if the decision had already been made by someone else to get rid of her once whatever they were doing was done.

She moved slowly down the corridor and eventually came across a pair of double doors. She looked through the window in the door; there was a brightly lit corridor containing five doors and another pair of double doors at the far end.

Her choice now was to turn back or go through. If she turned back, she would have achieved nothing by breaking out of her room. On the other hand, if she went through, she would have reached the point of no return—she would have to go right on to the end.

"Sod it," she muttered under her breath and pushed the doors open.

Gillien stepped into the corridor. She glanced in the rooms as she went along the corridor. When she reached the middle room, she stopped and peered through the window in the door. She saw six people in six hospital beds; they were all hooked up to monitors measuring their vital signs. She wondered if these were the people that they were experimenting on. She wanted to stop and take a closer look, see what they were doing, even try to identify who they were experimenting on. She made a grab for the door handle, but then thought it could be alarmed to warn them of intruders. She let go of the door handle. She wanted to go in but couldn't afford to get caught. If she got out, then that would be for Leanne to sort out. She carried on along the corridor and went through the next set of doors; there were steps that lead downwards.

It cannot be this easy, surely, she though as she descended down the steps. She came to a short landing and could hear people coming up the stairs. There was a door to her right; she went through the door.

She found herself in an auditorium. Looking towards the stage, she could see three men in white coats talking to Taylor. She moved back a couple of rows, crouched down between two chairs, and peered over the top. The door opened, and two more men entered the auditorium and went down to the front. Gillien recognised both men from when she was abducted from outside of the police headquarters. She bobbed low so that they wouldn't see her—something was about to happen.

She couldn't take them on herself; she needed to get help quickly. She peeped over the top of a seat and watched them go into the small room and out of sight. She crept silently towards the door, then slipped quietly out, back on to the landing, and proceeded down the steps. She found herself at the main door. She tried the handle; the door was not locked, and she stepped outside. It had just started to rain.

She ran across the courtyard to the main gates. They were locked. She tried the little door in the gate—this was also locked. She was now getting wet from the steady rainfall. She looked around the yard and found an overcoat neatly folded in one corner. She went over to the overcoat and picked it up. Beneath the coat was a home-made grappling hook. She looked around, surprised: was someone trying to help her to escape? Everything had gone far too easily—no one had tried to stop her, and then to find this here? It was too much of a coincidence.

She put on the overcoat. It was much too big for her, but at least it would keep her dry.

She carried the grappling hook to the gate and threw it up. It clanked against the metal doors. She tried again and again and again. On the sixth or seventh go it went over the top. She pulled on the rope—it snagged. Her arms were now aching, and she was getting tired. She tried to scramble up the gates, but her feet slipped on the wet metal. She wrapped her legs around the rope, pulled herself up on the rope, and was eventually able to grab the top of the gate. She hauled herself up.

Gillien couldn't believe it was this easy to escape—no one had tried to stop her getting out. She wondered if they were letting her go, if they needed to let her go, or if Taylor had kept to his word and let her get out before they killed her.

She lowered herself down the other side and dropped to the ground. The rain was coming down harder. She put her hands in the coat pocket and found a beanie hat. She put this on—it would keep her hair dry. Her hands were cold; she wished that they had left her some gloves in the other pocket, but it wasn't to be.

She needed to get the information that she had gathered back to Leanne. She set off at a pace back to the police station.

Gillien looked up—she was standing outside a café on Nelson Lane. *How did I get here?* she thought. *This is not where I want to be.*

Gillien looked around; there was no one about. She set off again for the police station.

When she got there, the police station was empty. *This is not right*, she thought.

Gillien went upstairs to Timpson's office. Again there was no one around. She called out for Leanne, but there was no reply. She went to Leanne Best's desk—there was a route map for Fenton's walkabout. "It's today," she said out aloud to no one in particular.

Gillien then went back outside. The clouds had parted and the rain had stopped, but it was still overcast, although the sun was trying to get out. Gillien took off the heavy overcoat, folded it up, and placed it on the steps outside the station. She then dashed towards the town centre—she needed to get to the square before anything happened.

She approached the town square, where a large crowd had gathered. She pushed her way through. There seemed to be some kind of commotion in the square, and people were starting to leave. Then she saw Wayne Taylor, tears in his eyes. She manoeuvred her way over to him.

"Taylor," she called out.

Wayne Taylor turned towards her. "It's too late," he said. "We're too late."

Gillien turned towards the square. Something had happened in the square—there were bodies lying on the ground. She turned again to Taylor, but he was gone.

CHAPTER 24

DISCOVERY

Today was the last day of the tour. Daniel Hobson had been Timpson's driver on four of the dates, Lisa Barber had been the driver on four dates, and now Glen Morris was out on his fourth time as Timpson's driver. Although no driver was needed today, Leanne believed from the clues she had got from Taylors house that he would try to shoot Fenton from the clock tower. So Timpson despatched Morris to the clock tower and told him to look out for Taylor. Morris was told to be vigilant, and also to look out for anyone wearing bright-yellow ear protectors.

Lisa Barber was out investigating an incident down by the canal, Morris was in town with Best and Timpson, Daniel had been left in the office to babysit for Holly, she was now fully recovered but Leanne was protective of her and wanted to keep her out of harm's way whilst Taylor was still on the prowl.

In the past Hobson would not have enjoyed this but with Leanne's words still ringing in his ears that she trusted him he now for the first time that he was a part of the team and after having had the shared dream with Holly meadows that had also now connected

Hobson looked across at Meadows; she was writing up the report on the attack on Hamilton. They still had not made an arrest. Gary Taylor was still the main suspect, but they didn't have enough evidence. Leanne Best was the only one who had seen him in the last few days, and he had got away from her. They were no nearer to getting him than they were on day one.

The phone rang and Hobson answered. It was Lisa Barber. She asked if Meadows was in.

"Yeah, she's in," he replied and handed the phone to Meadows.

"Hi, Lisa, what's up?"

"We've found something down by the canal. I think you need to come down here."

"We cannot come out at the moment."

"I think this will help you solve the case with Adam Hamilton."

Meadows looked across to Hobson.

"We need to go," she said.

Hobson reached across and pulled a device called a portcullis, normally a portcullis is a big gate on a castle that cannot be opened this device opens any deadlock ever made no matter how strong the door or gate maybe, it creates a magnetic image of a key and remotely un-opens the lock, Daniel had never used the device but has a feeling that today was going to be the day when he would need it, he picked up the device from the corner of his desk and put it in his pocket. Hobson and Meadows went down to where the canal towpath had access to the main street, just a few yards from where Taylor lived. Two ambulances and a forensic-unit van were already parked when they got there They went down to the canal towpath, and a hundred or so yards along, they could see a white forensics tent. Another hundred yards along, and set back from the towpath they could see Lisa Barber waiting for them.

They rushed on to meet her. "It's not a pretty sight," Lisa said.

"What do we have?" Holly asked.

"We have two bodies."

"Do we know who?"

"We believe it to be La' Court and her lover, the magician Mr Magica."

"Do we know how long they have been here?" Hobson asked.

"Forensics estimates they have been here anywhere between six and eight years."

"Roughly around the time Taylor's father was killed and about the time Taylor said she left him," Meadows mused.

Meadows turned to Hobson. "We need to go and see him."

Hobson had been expecting this, and that's why he had picked up the portcullis from his desk. They walked back up the towpath to Taylor's house.

Meadows tried the door—it was still locked. She banged on the door and called through the letter box, "Police, open up." There was no response.

Hobson took the portcullis out of his pocket this was a dish of four inches in diameter with a red button in the middle, he placed the device over the lock and pressed the button it whirred for a moment as it generated a virtual skeleton key then click the lock opened

Daniel Hobson opened the door and stood back to let Holly Meadows go in first. Holly took a tentative step inside; there was a musty smell which suggested that Taylor had not been staying here for some while. There were bills piled up on the floor behind the door. Meadows picked them up and placed them neatly on the little phone table in the hallway. Hobson followed her into the house.

"Armed police, show yourself." Meadows called out. Again there was no reply.

Meadows opened the door to the living room. There was still no sign of Taylor. Hobson climbed the stairs towards the bedroom.

Holly Meadows strode through the living room and entered the kitchen. On the kitchen table, five bullets stood on their ends—like soldiers on parade, they were standing to attention, ready to be inspected. Meadows let out a little shriek when she saw the bullets standing there. Hobson rushed into the kitchen.

"He's got a gun," Meadows said.

Hobson noticed some hand-drawn diagrams on the table. They were not of the square but of Wellington Street and Washington Road. The details confused Meadows and Hobson—unless Taylor was deliberately setting a false trail to lure them away from the square.

"We need to see Leanne," Holly said.

Meadows and Hobson left the house and drove down to the square. They had to pull up some distance from the square, as a big crowd was gathering. They would need to walk the last bit of the way.

Fenton was about to make his way out to do his last walkabout and meet the crowd of adoring fans, which would see him get another term in office. At the far end of the square, a group of children dressed as majorettes were getting ready to perform for Fenton. Young Alice, aged just six, stood at the front with a collage that they had made. She was to present this to Fenton.

Morris was in the clock tower scouring the crowd with a pair of binoculars. There was no sign of Taylor. He scanned the crowd from left to right; still there was no sign of Taylor, but he did see Hobson and Meadows working their way through the crowd.

———————————

Holly Meadows and Daniel Hobson reached the back of the crowd. They could not see their way through to the front. Hobson pointed to the far end of the square. "You go left, I'll go right," he said.

Daniel Hobson pushed his way through the crowd. Moving to the right, he reached the front. He could see Fenton getting ready to make his entrance. Alexander Timpson and his brother, Jonathan, were with him. Giving last minute instructions behind them, he could just see Luke Appleyard and Leanne Best. He needed to get through but was crushed against a barrier—with people pushing from behind, he could not move any further.

To the left, Holly Meadows pushed through the crowd making little headway. If she had studied his picture, she would have recognised Wayne Taylor as she pushed past him.

She could hear the children singing as they entered the square. She pushed her way through to the front and saw the majorettes marching and singing the song. Alice was at the front with the collage; to either side of her were two older girls twirling batons. The crowd cheered as the girls entered the square. Then, from the other end of the square, Fenton entered waving his arms in the air, flanked on either side by the Timpson brothers. Behind him came Appleyard and Best.

Then the crowd went silent. Entering the square, behind the children, was Gary Taylor. He was holding out a gun in front of him and walking towards Fenton. Holly Meadows drew out her gun. In the distance, she heard Leanne Best call out, "Armed police; put down your weapon."

Gary Taylor still continued to march forward with his gun pointing right at Matt Fenton. Children started to scream and scatter. Leanne called out again. "Armed police; put down your weapon."

CHAPTER 25

EXECUTION

Timpson and Best were at the entrance of the square waiting for Fenton and his party to arrive to start the final leg of his grand tour. So far it had been an unprecedented success—far better than he could have wished for. Timpson expected something to happen today; this would be Taylor's last chance to get Fenton. Timpson had placed many officers in the square, with Morris sitting in the clock tower scanning the crowd with a pair of binoculars. Several other officers were dotted around the place just to be on the safe side. They were all looking out for Gary Taylor. All the officers were armed, and all carried a picture of Taylor. This was the last stage of Fenton's grand tour. If anything was going to happen, it would have to be today, here in the square.

Timpson stood nervously looking up at the clock in the big tower across the square. *Get today over and done*, he thought, *and I will have completed my mission.* Then Timpson would be a happy man, he just needed today to go by without a hitch. The sun was shining; the ground was still damp from the earlier downpour, but apart from that, everything was bright. Surely it was too much to hope for that Taylor was not going to attack Fenton today.

Fenton was in the mayor's chambers outlining his plans for the future. Only a few minutes more and he would be out for his final walkabout. Timpson looked across to Inspector Best. She nodded to him to indicate that everything was fine.

There was a large crowd gathering in the square, probably the biggest of the whole tour. Morris had been paced up in the clock tower; he had a perfect view of the whole square. He scanned around the edges—everything was calm and still. There was an anticipation amongst the crowd as they waited for Fenton to appear.

The crowd suddenly went quiet. Hushed whispers said Fenton was here, coming from the north end of the square. He appeared, flanked on either side by Alexander and Jonathan Timpson. Behind them was Luke Appleyard with Leanne Best by his side. Fenton walked into the square and held up his hand. The crowd cheered and waved. This was by far the biggest crowd that had gathered during the tour, and they were the noisiest too. Fenton was lapping it up; he waved to the crowd and they cheered again.

Across the other side of the square, the majorettes entered singing the song about the grand old duke. In the front was six-year-old Alice. She carried the collage of Fenton that the children had done for the occasion. She was to present it to Fenton in the middle of the square. Alice was flanked by two older girls twirling their batons.

Fenton turned to Appleyard. "This is what we want. If we can stir the crowd up like this again when the election comes around, we will walk it back in."

The majorettes marched toward Fenton. The crowd cheered and waved. Morris could still not see Taylor in the crowd, but he spotted Hobson and Meadows meandering through the crowd.

The sun was shining after the morning rains. This had turned out to be a bright afternoon. Fenton had triumphed again; everyone was happy. Suddenly, there was a commotion at the other end of the square. Fenton, Appleyard, and Jonathan Timpson seemed to be unaware of what was going on and continued to wave to the crowd. The crowd went quiet as Taylor entered the square at the far end, holding out a gun in front of him. He marched towards Fenton.

Leanne Best shouted out a warning. "Armed Police, put down your weapon."

Gary Taylor walked towards Matt Fenton. He had a gun taped to his right hand—he could not put down his weapon. He held the gun out in front of him. He could not move his arm; it was held level, pointing forwards. His other arm swung backwards and forwards; his mouth was gagged—he could not call out. Tears rolled down his eyes; he wanted to stop, but he was not in control of his own body.

Leanne Best called out again. "Armed police, put down your weapon."

Gary Taylor did not respond. He continued to walk forwards with his gun stretched out before him. The children screamed and started to scatter.

There was a loud crack, and a bullet thundered into Taylor's shoulder, rocking his upper body backwards. But he continued to walk forward pointing the gun at Fenton.

Another bullet sliced through the sleeve of his left arm, and another tore into his left leg. Two more bullets pounded into his chest, and another ripped through his arm. It was like he was being stung by a swarm of bees as the bullets continued to hit him. One after another thudded into his chest. He dropped to his knees, and the bullets still hit him. He closed his eyes, rolled forward, and lay on the ground in a pool of blood.

Leanne Best's face lit up. "We've done it. We've stopped him and saved Fenton."

She turned to face Timpson; the colour had drained from his face. Fenton lay beside him with a single bullet wound in the middle of his forehead. Beside him lay the six-year-old Alice, still holding on to the collage. In the crowd, Daniel Hobson and Holly Meadows stood with smoking guns. Both had fired vital shots, but neither could remember who they had shot at.

Panic spread through the crown they started to run out departing in all directions knocking into each other as they went pushing and jostling for the exits, three men down, or to be more precise, two men and a little girl down.

Julie Gillien stepped through the crowd into the square, the horror of what had just happened etched across her face. She wondered, if she had escaped the day before, if she could have stopped this from happening.

An ambulance rolled into the square. Gillien approached Best and Timpson; Best looked the worst for wear and tear. There was no sign of Morris.

Daniel Hobson climbed the clock tower. There he found Morris lying on the floor with a plank of wood beside his body. He had been knocked cold before the shooting started. Hobson and a constable from the met carried Morris down to the waiting ambulance. He would be taken to hospital to be checked out. When he came round, Morris remembered nothing of what had happened: he had seen Hobson and Meadows enter the crowd and work their way to the front, but then everything went blank until he came around in the ambulance.

Timpson gathered his troops and took them back to the station. The whole operation had been an unmitigated disaster. Their only objective was to see that Fenton completed the tour in one piece, but he had been killed outright with a single bullet to the head, right in front of their noses. They had taken out Taylor, but an innocent bystander—the young girl, Alice—had also perished.

Timpson knew that his department would have to take the rap for this. On the plus side, they had got Gillien back, and she had news on Wayne Taylor and the psionic neuro integrator. Timpson insisted that Gillien should come with them when they went to the Corporation, but first he insisted that she go home, have a shower, and get changed.

Leanne drove Gillien home. On the way, Gillien told her what she had learned—that she thought Wayne Taylor was a good man, but the people running the Corporation were corrupt and stealing his idea, which was created to help people. The Corporation had turned it into a weapon instead, and this was not what he had intended to use it for.

Gillien had a hot shower, her first for nearly four weeks—it felt good. She changed and they went back to the station.

Timpson was eagerly awaiting their return. They would take two cars: Timpson would be in the lead car with Hobson, with two constables from the met. In the second car would be Leanne Best, Meadows, Gillien, and Lisa Barber.

They drove down to the Corporation. The green doors were wide open. They drove into the courtyard. Hobson and Barber stayed by the cars just in case anyone came out.

Gillien led them in through the front door of the Corporation. She took them up the stairs; they went past the auditorium, along the corridor, up the next set of stairs, through the double doors, and on to the third door in the corridor. She felt for the light switch and turned on the light. The room was empty—they had cleared it out. Gillien looked around as surprised as anyone. "They've gone," she said.

Timpson had his officers check every room. The Corporation had gone—there was no sign that they had ever been there at all.

They went back to the station. Timpson got every one of his team to write a report about their involvement on the case. He gathered all the information and put it in a file entitled "The Corporation", then put the file in a sealed envelope to which only he had the access codes.

CHAPTER 26

GOODBYE MY LOVE

Wayne and Martha Taylor had been called to Stancer Memorial Hospital, their son had been in a coma for seven years now he was slipping away it looked like he had given up on life. All was pandemonium, nurses were rushing around here there and everywhere, the doctors looked over the lifeless body of Gary Taylor. He had been in a coma since the car crash seven years ago and he had never recovered consciousness now he seemed to have given up the fight and was slowly slipping away. His girlfriend, Vivianne La' Court, hugged his mother, Martha Taylor. They both wept as the doctors told them that he was going and there was nothing else that they could do for him.

His father, Wayne Taylor, paced the floor anxiously. "Can't you do anything for my boy?" he asked the doctor.

"There doesn't appear to be anything we can do," a doctor replied. "It looks like he has given up fighting for his life."

Three doctors had taken the primary care for Gary Taylor whilst he was in a coma. Dr Bishop was the oldest—he was balding and what little hair he had around the edges had already turned grey. Dr Knight wore horn rimmed glasses and Dr Castle had a goatee. They had spent many a night during the last seven years sitting around Gary Taylor's bed, talking to him, trying to encourage him to awake from the coma. Now it looked like Taylor had given up the fight, and he was not coming back,

Wayne Taylor looked down on his son, whose life was slipping away from him. "Surely there is something you can do," he pleaded with the doctors.

"We've done everything we can do for the last seven years. It's down to him now. It may be best that he passes peacefully, as after all this time, we do not know what condition he will be in and what quality of life he will have if he did recover," said Dr Bishop.

Martha Taylor burst into tears again. The nurse, Rose Wilson, tried to comfort her. "You know, I used to see him nearly every day. I would sit outside the café on Nelson Lane after my shift, and he would walk past me every evening on his way home from work. I don't think he ever saw me. He never spoke to me, not even once. It was like I was invisible to him."

Family and friends sat around his bed talking about the good times that they had had with Gary.

"He had an irrational fear of clowns you know," his mother said.

"Yes, I know, you've told me many times before," Vivianne replied.

"It's a good job that you work for that magician then and not a circus clown. He would be having a fit."

They all laughed. The monitor stopped blipping—it flat lined. Wayne Taylor looked across to doctor Bishop he came over and felt for a Pulse, "he's gone," the doctor said

---

Seven days later, Gary Taylor was buried at the City Road Cemetery. There were not many people at the funeral. Mr and Mrs Taylor were there as was the nurse, Rose Wilson. The three doctors came as did his boss, Chris Rothberry, his former workmate Domenic Clarkson, his former flatmate, Craig Marksbrow, and his girlfriend, Vivianne La' Court.

Also in attendance representing the police; Inspector Leanne Best and WPC Holly Meadows, they had been the officers on duty that day. They had responded to the RTA and had given first aid to Gary at the scene of the accident. That was all the people that were there to say a final goodbye to Gary Taylor.

Wayne Taylor approached Vivianne. "What are you going to do now?" he asked her.

"Magica has got a summer season with Tinky at Blackpool. I will be up there for the summer. After that, who knows."

In a black limousine parked at a discrete distance, two men sat in the back watching the proceedings. "How are Lord Malcolm's plans for the universal credit coming along?" asked Nathaniel Watson.

"I will see to it that it never gets government approval," Matt Fenton replied.

They watched as the coffin was lowered into the ground. "It's a good job it ended this way," said Fenton. "With what Taylor had found out, he could have ruined everything. He could have stopped us financing the Corporation before it even started, and we couldn't have allowed that."

"It wouldn't have done your political aims much good either," Watson responded. "I'm surprised no one ever checked the breaks or the steering on Taylor's car."

"My men took care of that."

"What if it comes out now that he's died?"

"Nothing will come out. We have a way of burying the truth. No one will ever know that the crash was not an accident."

"That's good. With the right backing, you will go far in this government."

"I hope to be prime minister one day."

With that Fenton ordered the driver to move on—they wanted to get out before the funeral party departed. They drove past a blue car parked up on the side of the road.

Vivianne paid her last respects to Gary. "Goodbye, my love," she said and walked out to the waiting car.

Wayne Taylor saw a tall blonde woman standing in the shadows. He approached her cautiously. "Did you know my son?" he asked

"No," she replied.

"Then can I ask you what you are doing here at my son's funeral?"

"I was driving the other car that your son drove into. He killed my little girl—she was just six years old and a drum majorette. We were just coming back from her first group practice. Your son drove into us and took my little girl away from me."

Wayne Taylor apologised for his son's actions and tried his best to comfort the blonde woman. "I just wanted to know why he did it," she said. "He drove straight at us."

"That, my dear, we will never know—now that he has gone."

He led the woman from the cemetery. The woman sobbed uncontrollably for the first time in seven years. Taylor didn't know if she cried for her daughter or because his son had passed away without giving her the answers that she so desperately needed.

Lightning Source UK Ltd.
Milton Keynes UK
UKHW012006261021
392884UK00001B/18